Gail needed a dictionary to find out what disruptive meant, but it didn't sound good. She recognized that she deserved a reprimand, but so did someone else. Mr. Addison didn't care about that. Knowing she was throwing fuel on the fire but too angry to care, she said, "I'll be glad to apologize in homeroom, right after whoever put that egg in my chair apologizes to me."

He threw up his hands. "You will not dictate conditions, young lady. I will deal with the prankster as I see fit, not as you wish."

Gail would have bet her chicken money no one else would be punished. She pressed her lips together to hold back the words.

"What do you have to say?"

Gail considered giving in, but she'd never been good at that. "I've said what I have to say."

THE FEEDSACK DRESS

CAROLYN MULFORD

A Cave Hollow Press Book

Warrensburg, Missouri   2007

The Feedsack Dress

Copyright © 2007 by Cave Hollow Press
ISBN 0-9713497-4-6
ISBN 978-0-9713497-4-2

Cover art by Georgia R. Nagel

Except for short passages used in critical articles or reviews, no part of this book may be reproduced or transmitted in any form or by any means, electronic or mechanical, including photocopying, recording, or by any information storage and retrieval system, without permission in writing from the publisher. For information, write:
Cave Hollow Press
304 Grover
Warrensburg, MO 64093.

Cave Hollow Press
Warrensburg, MO

10 9 8 7 6 5 4 3 2 1

Acknowledgments

Many people helped me as I wrote and rewrote and rewrote *The Feedsack Dress*.

Family: The oldest generation assisted in reconstructing daily life on the farm and in junior high in 1949. The youngest generation let me know what they couldn't comprehend from the past and what plagues kids in the present.

Critique group: Although focused on mysteries for adults, the group—Barb, John, Mary, and Tim—graciously included this project in our weekly sessions. They helped me clarify many points as they commented, chapter by chapter, on a final revision.

Friends: Joyce went over this manuscript almost as many times as I did, giving me guidance and encouragement each time. Detta not only read it but also found two perceptive teenagers to give objective feedback. Other enthusiastic readers included members of the Washington, D.C., Alpha Sigma Alpha alumnae chapter.

Thanks to all my work-in-progress readers for sharing memories, reactions, and suggestions. Writers work alone, but readers spur them on.

THE FEEDSACK DRESS

Chapter One

"Not even one left?" Gail Albright couldn't hide her disappointment. She'd counted on buying her chicken feed in a cotton sack with morning glories on a white background. She needed another sack to have enough material for a dress.

"I'm mighty sorry, Gail," the feedstore owner said. "That pattern's been awful popular with the ladies. I sold out the day it came in."

Gail's father paused on his way to the pickup with a block of cattle salt. "Do you figure to get any more, Harry?"

The feedstore owner shook his bald head. "I don't think so, Simon. They're just not makin' many feedsacks with pretty patterns anymore. Folks ain't usin' them the way they did during the Depression and the war. But I'll sure watch for one for you. How about takin' a sack of chicken feed with

Chapter One

the white daisies on blue? That's right pretty."

Gail sighed. "Yes, Mom has one of those. She means to make herself a dress from it. I guess that'll have to do."

"Now, honey," her father said, "you get what you want. You're the one goin' to a new school next week."

Gail swallowed the lump in her throat. "Not really anything else here I want."

Simon Albright picked up a sack of feed with the daisy pattern. "All right, then. You go get yourself a bottle of pop while Harry and I load the feed." He turned to the older man. "She's pretty near as good a fieldhand as a man. Guess she's earned a drink on a hot August afternoon."

Mr. Holt nodded toward the small grocery attached to his feedstore. "Got some pop on ice. My granddaughter is watching the store for me to earn a little extra money. She'll be a ninth grader this year, too. Of course, the junior high won't be new to her. She's gone there the last two years."

Excited to meet a future classmate, Gail stepped through the screen door into the grocery. In front of the counter stood a teenager who looked like the models in the Sears and Roebuck catalog. Wearing a low-necked white blouse and a full yellow skirt that came only two or three inches below her knees, she had turned so an electric fan blew her long, wavy, blonde hair out behind her.

The girl's fashionable outfit reminded Gail she'd come to town straight out of the field without cleaning up and changing clothes. She wished she were wearing a freshly

The Feedsack Dress

starched skirt and blouse instead of one of her father's old blue chambray shirts with the sleeves cut off, paper thin blue jeans rolled up to her knees, and penny loafers so scuffed you couldn't tell whether they were brown or black. She reached up to untie the two binder-twine bows that held her uncurled shoulder-length, brown hair off her neck just as the girl noticed her standing in the door.

"May I help you?" the girl asked mechanically. She didn't return Gail's shy smile.

"I'd like a grape pop, please."

"Help yourself." The girl picked up a magazine and began flipping through it. She didn't look up as Gail dropped her nickel in the shoe box by the big red cooler, opened the lid, and took the bottle floating by the biggest block of ice.

Gail used the opener built into the cooler and pushed a strand of hair back from her damp forehead. "Your grandpa said you'll be a freshman this year. So will I. I'm Gail Albright."

The girl lifted her eyes from her magazine and stared at Gail a long moment. "I'm Veronica Holt," she finally announced.

"Gee, Veronica is just the right name for you. Your hair falls over your face just like that movie star, Veronica—umm—"

"Lake," the girl said, her eyes once again on her magazine.

Gail wondered if she should just leave, but she took a drink of pop and tried again. "What are ya readin'?"

Chapter One

"I'm reading"—she emphasized the "g"—"*Harper's Bazaar.*" She looked up from the magazine. "I'm planning my school wardrobe. Mother and I are going to St. Louis to shop this weekend, and I don't want to waste my time on last year's styles."

"You—you buy all your clothes in St. Louis?" Gail didn't know anyone who did that. Even her aunt who worked in a huge office building in Chicago made most of her own clothes.

"Certainly!" Veronica said as though insulted at the thought she would shop anywhere else. "Oh, you saw those." She pointed to two or three empty feedsacks with the morning glory pattern lying on the counter. "I wouldn't have a housecoat made out of that coarse cotton." She shuddered. "Grandmother is going to make tea towels. Only dirt-poor farmers use feedsacks for clothes these days."

Hurt and angry, Gail bit back a denial. Feeling the blood move up her neck and redden her cheeks, she finished her pop in one long swig and mumbled, "I'll see you at school next week."

Without waiting for an answer, Gail rushed out to the Albrights' battered red pickup. She stood on the running board an instant to look into the back to make sure her father had remembered the grit for her chickens. Then she climbed into the cab and, aware her face still glowed, avoided her father's eyes.

"Don't worry, Gail," he said as he forced the gearshift

into first. "We won't send you to school naked."

Gail couldn't smile at his little joke. "Maybe it's just as well that Mr. Holt ran out of that feedsack."

He glanced at her in surprise. "What makes you say that?"

"I don't think the town kids wear feedsack dresses to school."

"Well, I reckon they don't buy feed, so they don't have feedsacks." He frowned. "Old man Holt's granddaughter tell you that?"

"She said that only poor people make clothes out of feedsacks. She made it sound—shameful. The big snob buys all her clothes in St. Louis."

Her father gripped the steering wheel so hard his knuckles turned white. "Gail, there's no shame in wearin' what you can afford, long as it's clean. We're not rich, but we're not poor neither. Why, we'll finish payin' off the farm in five years, if those years are as good as 1948 was. You know we'd like you to have store-bought dresses, but we won't have any cash to spare until after we shuck corn and pay off the fertilizer loan in October."

She'd heard this before. "I know, but maybe if I get top price for my hens, I could buy just one dress. My pullets will be big enough to sell as layers in a couple weeks."

He shook his head. "No use foolin' yourself. You got to have shoes and paper and pencils for school, not to mention a winter coat. That's what we got you the hundred baby

Chapter One

chicks for. You're old enough to understand that a farmer buys only what he can't produce for himself."

Gail felt ashamed. She was acting like Bobby, her nine-year-old brother, instead of a teenager who had done a man's work in the fields all summer. "I understand, Dad. Let's not say anything to Mom about it."

As soon as they unloaded the feed, Gail headed for the corncrib to shell corn to supplement the feed they'd bought in town. Since the last harvest she'd almost emptied the crib. She liked coming here. Dislodging the bright yellow grains from the cobs into a rusty bucket kept her hands busy and her mind free. Even better, Bobby wouldn't come near her for fear of being put to work, and the grains hitting the tin bucket made so much noise she couldn't hear her mother call her from the house.

The shelling couldn't stop her from thinking, though, that a feedsack dress would have labeled her a hick or, even worse, poor. Clothes hadn't been a problem at the nearby one-room school she'd attended for eight years. All fifteen students had worn hand-me-downs, homemade clothes, or jeans.

A wet tongue on her left hand interrupted her thoughts and her work. She patted the head of the short-haired black and white mongrel seeking her attention and then gently pushed him away. "Run along, Ratter. I've got to finish this corn, and"—she straightened her shoulders and tossed her head as though her hair were long and glamorous—"I've got to plan my school wardrobe."

"That's about all your pea brain can handle," Bobby said from behind her. "Good thing you only got two skirts and two blouses to choose from. Mom says to come on to supper so you'll have time to let down the hem of that ugly brown skirt Aunt Ellen sent before it gets dark."

She tossed a cob at him. "Soon as I finish this ear. You go ahead and start washing. Maybe you can get the topsoil off your face by the time I get there."

While she finished, she wondered what to tell her mother about her talk with Veronica, but Flo Albright, busy putting dishes on the table, didn't say anything when Gail came into the kitchen. Gail stayed silent as she dipped water from the bucket into the yellow enamel washbasin and scrubbed her deeply tanned face. She glanced at her father, already at the table, and he looked away.

"Harry had some good news today, Flo," he said as Gail's mother took her place at the oak table. "The electrical co-op expects to have all the wires up and turn on our electricity by the first of November. We'll need to hire the Kruger boys to wire the house and barn at the end of October."

"Can't be too soon for me," she said, glaring at the huge wood-burning stove that dominated the roomy kitchen.

"Me neither." He buttered a thick slice of bread fresh from the oven. "I figure I'll be able to milk twenty cows by machine in the time it takes us both to milk ten by hand

Chapter One

now. Soon as we sell the corn, I'm goin' to buy a couple of Ed's Tennessee Jersey heifers. They make right good milkers."

Bobby helped himself to a cold fried chicken wing and half a dozen slices of the tomatoes he had just brought in from the garden. "With an electric radio we can listen to that new Craigsburg radio station all we want."

"It'll sure be nice to have a good light to study by," Gail said.

Her mother nodded. "And sew by. Si, we need lots of things more than those pricey cows."

"Those cows will pay for themselves by summer," Simon argued. "Besides, we need the wood stove for heat this winter. We'll get you an electric stove next summer, if we have enough left after we get the crops in."

She glanced at Gail. "I wasn't thinkin' just of the stove, Si."

He frowned. "Gail will buy what she needs with her chicken money."

Gail was relieved to hear the phone jingle out their ring, two longs and two shorts.

Her mother hurried into the living room and lifted the earpiece off the wooden box on the wall. "Hello," she called into the mouthpiece. "Yes, this is Flo Albright." She listened a minute or so. "How very kind. Thank you so much. We'll pick it up Saturday when we come in to do the tradin'."

She returned to the kitchen with a step as light as

when she had begun work twelve hours earlier. "Good news, Gail. Harry Holt found a morning glory feedsack. His wife had one she doesn't need. Isn't that wonderful?"

Gail couldn't believe her bad luck. She looked at her dad. He was smiling as he put a big bite of potato salad on his fork. "That's just great, Mom." She hid her face behind a chicken leg. "Just great."

Chapter Two

"Get up, Gail," her mother called. "I want to fit your dress before we go to Sunday school. It's goin' to rush us something fierce to finish making it today."

Gail groaned. She'd never finish it if she had her way. But she wouldn't. She steeled herself to hide her hatred for the dress. She even practiced looking happy in the clear part of the mirror over her old oak dresser.

Her mother hurried in with the pieces they had cut out by the light of the kerosene lamp Saturday night. "This new dress pattern is going to make up real pretty, honey, especially with those blue-violet morning glories matching your eyes. Slip the top over your head and climb up on a chair so I can pin on the skirt."

Gail turned all the way around as least five times while her mother pinned the pieces to fit.

At last Gail's mother stood back to study the effect. "That looks good, but I 'spect we should leave it a little big. Fast as you've grown this past year, I wouldn't be surprised if you'll need a little extra room soon."

Gail couldn't stand it. "Aw, Mom, I'll look like a scarecrow if it's too big."

"I suppose you're right." She removed the pins from the bodice where the buttons would go. "I know you'd like to have a nice ready-made dress, and I'd like for you to have one. But your father's right. We have to buy only the things we can't make. Lots of girls wear feedsacks to school, and not many dresses will be as pretty as yours."

"I know, Mom. I don't mind."

But Gail did mind. Standing at the end of the driveway Monday morning clutching her new ring-binder notebook, the little gray purse her aunt had sent her, and her paper lunch sack, she wished that she was wearing her aunt's mud-brown skirt and dingy white blouse instead of the freshly starched feedsack dress. When the dirty yellow bus pulled up, she prayed she wouldn't run into Veronica Holt at school that day.

"Here!" Alice Walton shouted from the back as Gail hesitated by the driver, unsure where to sit on the unfamiliar bus.

She grabbed the back of a seat to steady herself as the driver gunned the motor, sending a spray of gravel against the metal mailbox. Safe by Alice, Gail admired her

Chapter Two

longtime classmate. "You got a home permanent, and what a beautiful dress!"

"Thanks." Alice gazed with pride at the hundreds of tiny red and white checks in her full, gathered, gingham skirt. She smoothed the white Peter Pan collar. "I got it at Stella's Style Shop last week. Your dress is lovely, too. Your mom sews so good you'd never guess it's a feedsack dress."

Gail sighed. Everyone would know, just as Alice had.

Alice opened her notebook. "Let's compare our schedules. After being the only ones in our grade for eight years, it'll be scary if the school puts us in different classes."

Gail looked at their lists. "Not one together!"

"What's your schedule?" asked a long-legged, red-haired boy sitting across the aisle. His freckled face wore a banana-size grin.

Alice read off her schedule.

"I got the same math and general science classes. I'm Red Royce. Our farm's just east of Hungry Hollow School."

Gail and Alice introduced themselves, and Gail read her schedule. She and Red had drawn the same social studies and English classes.

The trio fell silent as the bus arrived in Craigsburg, population 8,694. The driver stopped at the senior high first, and all but seven students got off. Gail had seen the other ninth graders at countywide 4-H Club events but didn't really know any of them. Nevertheless, the 350 teenagers milling around the junior high's front door made the kids on her bus seem like old friends.

The seven stuck together as they stepped down from the bus and faced the glass-paned double doors of the monstrous two-story brick building.

"Hey! You kids from the bus," called a thin, pale man in a dark blue suit. He motioned to them from the top of the four steps leading to the doors. "Which bus do you ride?"

Silence.

He frowned. "Speak up."

Gail moved forward, "We're from northeast of town, East Center, Hungry Hollow, Radical Ridge, and New Hope districts mostly."

"That isn't what I asked."

Red's face turned so red his freckles almost disappeared. "I think the driver said we're on route four."

The man nodded and looked at a clipboard. "Albright, Abigail."

"Yes, that's me. I'm here," Gail stammered.

"*Here* will be sufficient. When you go inside, ask for Veronica Holt. She will show you to your classes today."

Gail barely held back a "Heck!" She went past him up the steps and pulled on one of the big doors, but it wouldn't budge. She yanked in vain on the other one, and dropped her notebook and lunch.

The man sighed. "Be patient, Abigail. I'll unlock the door in a moment and let you all in at once."

Standing three steps higher than everyone else, Gail

Chapter Two

felt as conspicuous as a fox in a flock of sheep.

Red stepped up beside her and whispered, "Don't let him get your goat."

Gail smiled. She was glad that she had to look up to meet Red's brown eyes. Lots of the boys stood eye to eye with her. A few looked up, but a few looked down.

"Here come the feedsacks," said a familiar voice inside the school.

Red bit his lip and stared at his feet.

"It's okay," Gail said, refusing to let Veronica ruin the day. "I don't care what she says about my dress."

He glanced at Gail in surprise. "Your dress is real purty. I think she meant my shirt. The brown dye doesn't cover all the Owens Flour label."

The man unlocked the door. "All new students come forward. I'm letting you in before the first bell today so your guides can show you the way to your homerooms."

Gail took a deep breath and put on her happy face, determined not to show Veronica the feedsack remark had hurt.

Leaning against the wall in a plaid dress, Veronica was devoting her full attention to a tall, muscular boy with curly black hair. She ignored Gail.

A skinny boy who came up only to Gail's chin asked her name and then said loudly, "Hey, Veronica, you got a customer."

Veronica tossed her long blonde hair back, gave Gail

a fake smile, and motioned for her to follow.

Gail walked behind her down a long gray corridor with big wooden doors opening to identical classrooms. To fulfill her obligation, Gail said as sincerely as she could, "Veronica, I'd like to thank you for the feedsack."

Without looking around, Veronica said, "It wasn't my idea. You really impressed my grandfather with your 'cute' binder-twine bows." She turned to study Gail. Her lip curled in disgust. "He even suggested I have a feedsack dress made for school."

Unsure what to say, Gail remained silent.

When they came to a corner, Veronica pointed down the hallway to the right. "Your locker is down there. This is our homeroom, 110. You come here first every morning."

The middle-aged woman at the teacher's desk smiled. "Come in."

Veronica smiled back. "This is one of our new students, Mrs. Ransler. I'm helping her find her way around today."

An electric bell shrilled, and the roar of seventh, eighth, and ninth graders' voices filled the halls.

As Veronica turned away to greet friends, Gail made her way to the back row. She had expected desks, but instead the room contained about thirty-five solid wood chairs, each with a broad arm on the right side to write on. She put her lunch on the shelf underneath and studied the teacher. Her short brown hair fell in soft waves around a pleasant face, and her lavender shantung silk dress fit her beautifully. Gail

Chapter Two

had never seen anyone except the traveling preacher's wife wear anything so elegant. Gail reflected that Veronica must approve of this teacher's wardrobe.

The students quieted when the bell rang again and the teacher rose.

"I'm Mrs. Ransler. I'll be seeing you twice a day, in homeroom and in social studies. Many of you I don't know, so to help me learn your names, I'm seating you alphabetically. We'll start in the front row with Addison, Oliver."

"O.T., please," said the short boy who'd called Veronica for Gail. "I'd hate to be confused with my old man."

Most of the students laughed, and Mrs. Ransler smiled.

"Albright, Abigail," the teacher continued.

Gail took the seat next to O.T. "Just Gail, please."

The teacher made a note. "Boyle, Noreen."

The girl on Gail's right raised her hand without taking her eyes from a story in a frayed issue of *Collier's*.

Gail covertly studied the girl who had figured out what seat she would be assigned. Although wearing jeans and a short-sleeved red blouse, Noreen looked older and more sophisticated than the other girls. It wasn't just that she'd left training bras behind her. Nor was it her long black hair, her plucked eyebrows, or the bright red lipstick that matched her fingernail polish. Noreen Boyle radiated self-confidence, or at least indifference to what others thought of her.

Gail glanced around. All the other girls wore skirts, and the only make-up seemed to be lipstick. She added it to her lists of things she needed to buy.

After calling the roll, Mrs. Ransler passed out forms for each student to fill out. Gail had barely finished when the bell rang.

"Hurry up," Veronica hissed as she walked by.

Handing in the forms, Gail hurried to keep her guide in sight. When they reached speech class, Gail sat in the front row in anticipation of being placed there.

This teacher, a young blonde woman in a red dress and red and white high heels, followed a different plan. She called roll without asking anyone to move. Then she perched on the edge of her desk. "I'm glad to see so many enthusiastic students. Because you're so eager, I'm going to permit each of you to make your first speech today."

Several students groaned, and Gail's heart beat faster.

"I don't expect the Gettysburg Address," the teacher said soothingly. "I just want to know who you are and hear what you did last summer. I'll start things off. I'm Miss Harlan. This summer I worked on my master's degree at Northeast Missouri State Teachers College. Then I spent two weeks at the Lake of the Ozarks. Now, who will volunteer to go next?"

No one breathed as she looked around the room.

"What a timid group, but that won't last." Her eyes stopped on Gail. "This young lady adorned with morning glories has just volunteered."

Gail rose uncertainly and faced the class. "I'm Gail Albright. I—I helped my parents on the farm last summer."

Chapter Two

She sat down quickly.

Miss Harlan wasn't satisfied. "Tell us what you did on the farm, Gail."

Gail struggled to her feet again, even more uncomfortable than the first time. "I helped in the fields, raking hay, shocking oats, things like that."

"And?"

"And I hoed the garden and gathered the eggs. I pumped an ocean of water for the cows." She thought for an instant and added with a touch of pride, "And I raised a hundred baby chicks of my own."

Someone in the second row giggled, and Gail sat down wondering what anyone could have found funny. She heard whispering behind her where Veronica was sitting.

"She *egged* them on," a boy said, and the whole class snickered.

Miss Harlan killed the laughter by picking the next "volunteer."

No one else amused the group until O.T. spoke. "I spent all summer praying," he said, and he remained solemn despite hoots and whistles. "But it didn't do any good. The school and I are both here."

He bowed to the applause as the bell rang.

Gail didn't spring up as the others did and almost lost sight of Veronica on the way to English class. The teacher, a stern, gray-haired woman named Miss Clegmyer, seated students alphabetically, and once again, Gail had O.T.

on the left and Noreen on the right. Red Royce ended up in the back row.

The teacher passed out heavy reading books and instructed students to write one-page essays on what they did last summer.

"Puk-puk-puk-puk," sounded from somewhere behind Gail.

O.T. winked at Gail and began writing with a devilish grin. She hadn't finished when he poked her with his pencil and pointed to his paper.

Obligingly she skimmed a wild tale of hunting tigers in Africa.

"Tigers live only in Asia," she whispered. "Otherwise it's great."

She completed her dull account of farm chores, wishing she had as much nerve as O.T.

"We have eight minutes left," the teacher said. "Let's hear two or three." She looked at Gail. "I believe you're new this year. Would you like to introduce yourself to the class by reading your paper?"

Not recognizing the question as an order, Gail said, "No, it's too dull."

Miss Clegmyer frowned.

"O.T.'s is much more interesting," Gail added when she realized her mistake. "Nobody wants to hear any more about raising chickens."

"I'd like to read my paper," said a voice in the back.

Chapter Two

It was Red. "Cattle are lots more interesting than chickens."

Moos and clucking came from several well-concealed mouths.

"That's enough!" Miss Clegmyer snapped. "You will not turn this classroom into a barnyard!"

After a moment of complete silence, Red asked, "Should I read my paper, ma'am?"

O.T. whispered to Gail, "That your boyfriend?"

Gail shook her head no, but her cheeks grew warm. She forced herself to listen without expression as Red read through his paper with the speed and intonation of a bumblebee.

"You go next, Noreen," the teacher ordered.

Noreen closed her magazine and read, "Last summer I took advantage of all the recreational facilities Craigsburg has to offer. All I did was lie in the sun."

Miss Clegmyer sighed. "That doesn't fill one page very well, Noreen."

"It didn't fill my summer very well either," Noreen said.

The bell rang.

"Turn in your papers with your name in the upper right-hand corner," Miss Clegmyer called over the scraping of chairs.

In the seconds it took Gail to write her name, Veronica vanished. Panic swept over Gail. She had no idea which way to go to find her next class.

Noreen cocked an eyebrow at her. "Whatsa matter, kid?"

Gail didn't like being called a kid, but she had more important things to worry about than that. "I—I don't know where algebra is."

"I'm going there. Tag along with me."

Once there, Noreen headed for the only empty seat in the back row. Slightly hurt at the obvious rejection, Gail took one of the empty seats in the second row.

The teacher, a tiny woman who looked older than Gail's grandmother, introduced herself as Mrs. Lancaster before passing out mimeographed diagnostic tests. Although Gail worked the arithmetic problems on the first two pages easily, the problems on the third page made no sense to her. The best she could tell, letters stood for numbers.

When the period ended, Gail waited at the door for Noreen. "Could you tell me where to find the lunchroom, please?"

"Natch. Come on. I go by the Jail on my way out."

"The Jail?"

"The girls' lunchroom." Noreen tossed her magazine in a wastepaper basket. "So her royal highness ran out on you. What's your first class after lunch?"

"Physical education."

"The gym is down the hall to the right."

Gail cheered up as she entered the girls' lunchroom, a seventh-grade math room. The grumpy man who'd been at the front door stood by the teacher's desk, but she didn't care when she saw Alice's familiar face and several country

Chapter Two

kids they knew from 4-H. The town kids there probably lived too far from school to walk home for lunch.

"Quiet, please," the man shouted over the girls' voices. "Here are the rules for you new students, and the old ones, too. You must be in here five minutes after the bell dismissing your third-period class, and you must not leave except to go to the restroom next door until the warning bell rings for the fourth-period class. You are each to clean up your own crumbs. I will not tolerate uncleanliness in this room. Please remember you are young ladies, and you are not to be seen or heard in the halls."

Gail opened her lunch bag as he strode from the room. "Now I know why Noreen called this the Jail. I don't see why we have to stay in here the whole noon hour. It's cooler outside."

"It's only forty-five minutes, really," Alice said. As usual, she accepted whatever was happening without question.

Gail, who questioned everything, took out her bologna sandwich, an apple, and two oatmeal cookies. "I guess we're not even supposed to go get a drink of water."

With all the new things to talk about, the lunch hour flew by. Afterwards, thanks to Noreen's directions, Gail found the gym immediately. She recognized a few girls from her morning classes, but they talked only to each other. The gym teacher, Mrs. Chapelli, assigned them lockers—actually wire baskets on metal shelves—for their gym clothes and threatened to fail them if they didn't have clean gym shorts and blouses every Monday. Then she passed out mimeographed sheets with questions on volleyball rules. Having never even seen a game, Gail didn't know a single answer. The only game she knew was baseball.

Tailing Veronica to general science, Gail wished she were back in the familiar walls of her one-room school where the teacher knew not only the names but also the personalities of her fifteen students.

To her surprise, the science teacher looked familiar. Gail remembered him coming to the farm two or three times to buy tomatoes and cream. His wife had been driving, and he never got out of the car. Gail's father said Jack Wilkins had lost a leg fighting the Germans in World War II and had trouble walking on his artificial limb.

He remained seated as he called the roll and outlined what he expected them to learn that year. When he asked for volunteers to pass out the textbooks, three boys sprang forward.

"Now that we've taken care of business," the teacher said, "let's speculate a little about where science is taking us in the next fifty years. What changes do you think we'll see by 2000?"

The tall, athletic boy who'd been talking to Veronica that morning waved his hand in the air. "I think we'll be able to live on the moon."

"Aw, you're nuts, Phil," the boy next to him scoffed.

Mr. Wilkins just smiled. "Other predictions?"

Chapter Two

"A cure for polio," a girl said.

"Television in every house instead of just the window of Acuff's Appliance Store," said another.

On and on they went. It was the only class Gail had enjoyed all day.

She lost sight of Veronica on the way to her last class, but since it was in her homeroom, she knew where to find it. She sat in the seat Mrs. Ransler had assigned her that morning and fumbled to put her armload of books on the shelf under the chair.

O.T. plopped down beside her. "Why didn't you put the morning books in your locker?"

Gail felt foolish. "I forgot I had one, and I brought a padlock for it, too."

Mrs. Ransler seated the students alphabetically again, and this time half were in the right seats.

"This is a sharp group, I see," the teacher said. "I'll expect a lot from you, and not just in the classroom. I hope several of you will participate in student government, and I require all of you to follow current events on the radio news. Who can tell me what international issues are in the news now?"

Veronica held up her hand. "Trouble with the communists in the Soviet Union and China."

"Good. And what are some of the big issues here?" She looked to the back of the room. "Red?"

He answered quickly and firmly: "Price supports for

farmers' crops and health insurance for everyone. President Truman says only three and a half million Americans have decent health insurance."

Mrs. Ransler beamed. "Excellent. You have supported your opinion with facts. I can see we're going to have a good year." She distributed textbooks and passed out a test on American government. When students groaned, she said, "I just want to see what you remember. You can leave as soon as you finish. The junior and senior high are both dismissing early today for faculty meetings."

The class cheered and fell to work.

After facing strange questions all day, Gail rejoiced when she saw familiar material. She knew every answer to the questions on American government, but the ones on the Constitution challenged her memory. Focusing on which amendment was which, she ignored the sounds of other students' leaving. When the bell rang, she and Mrs. Ransler were alone.

The teacher smiled as she took the paper. "I have to go to a faculty meeting, and you better hurry to catch your bus."

Gail gathered up her books. They filled her arms. Remembering she had a locker, she hurried down the hall until she came to her number. She thrust the books she didn't need inside and found her padlock.

The halls were empty as she rushed outside. No one stood at the curb. The only ones around were O.T. and a

Chapter Two

boy she didn't know. They were playing catch with a football.

"Where's my bus?" she asked O.T., dreading the answer.

He paused with his arm cocked to throw. "Gone with the wind."

CHAPTER THREE

"But it can't have gone!" Gail wailed. "The bell just rang."

O.T. tucked the ball under his arm. "Everybody else came out early. You know, you shouldn't take so much time on those diagnostic tests. It's better to make a low score so you can impress the teacher when you improve." He shifted the ball to the other hand. "Can you walk home?"

"It's seven miles." Gail blinked back tears. Her parents would be furious.

He tossed the ball from hand to hand. "Got a phone?"

"Sure, but both my parents are in the field." She thought a moment. "Bobby should be home any time." Gail headed back to the door. "I'll call him from the principal's office."

Chapter Three

The door wouldn't open.

The other boy gestured for O.T. to throw the ball. "The principal locked it so no one can go in."

"He's an awful man. I hate him!" Gail blurted.

O.T. tossed the ball in a high, wobbly arc. "You can use the phone booth by the candy shop across the street."

Gail hadn't brought any money, not even the nickel she needed for a phone call. Maybe she could call from the grocery store where her parents shopped, but that meant carrying her heavy textbooks a half mile across town.

Knowing of no other solution, she waved goodbye to the boys and walked to the sidewalk. Watching the ball, she almost ran into Noreen.

"Waiting for a ride?" Noreen asked and started to move on.

"I missed my bus," Gail said, unable to stop herself. "The principal locked the door, and I can't get back in to call my folks." She took a deep breath. She didn't want to let this poised girl see how upset she was.

"That bastard!"

Gail didn't know the word, but she recognized the tone.

"Never mind," Noreen said. "You can call from our store. It's right up the street."

"Gosh, thanks a lot."

Noreen shrugged and started across the street. They walked half a block in silence, Gail afraid to speak and say something childish.

"Here it is," Noreen said, looking Gail in the eye for the first time.

"Oh, sure," Gail said, reading the sign over the sagging screen door. "Boyle's Used Furniture. We've driven by here lots of times."

Noreen studied her a moment. "Well, this time you can go in instead of by. I got to get on home and fix supper so I can get ready for my date. See ya tomorrow."

"See ya," Gail echoed and stepped into the store.

"What can I sell you, ma'am?" A man with a stubbly growth of whiskers and hair as black as Noreen's was stretched out on a couch. His legs were so long that his feet hung over the arm. "A nice kitchen table, perhaps?"

Gail grinned as she pulled the screen door tight. The place already had enough flies buzzing around. "Noreen said that I could use your phone. I missed my bus and need to call my folks."

"Turn right at that ugly green chair," he said without moving. "The phone's on the counter."

To Gail's intense relief, Bobby answered the phone and promised to go right out to the field without his usual bargaining for a return favor.

As she came back to the front of the store, Mr. Boyle said, "Come rest on one of my magnificently comfortable bargains."

Gail started for a big overstuffed sofa.

"Not there. Not a decent spring in it. Try the blue

Chapter Three

chair." He sat up and swung his long legs to the floor. "So you're a friend of Noreen's. Didn't know she had any girlfriends. What's your name?"

Surprised but charmed, Gail sat down and told him her name.

"Farm out north of town?"

"That's right."

"I used to play in the Sunday baseball league with your dad. Before Pearl Harbor. Care for a beer?"

Gail laughed.

He shook his head in mock sorrow. "I hate to drink alone, but I hate worse not to drink at all. If you will excuse me . . ." He stood up slowly and wavered a moment before heading toward the back of the store.

Gail sat stunned. She'd seen a man drunk on the square one Saturday night. He'd moved that same awkward, careful way that Noreen's father did.

To spend the time, she read her English assignment, a story called "The Ransom of Red Chief." No one came into the store to interrupt her, and Mr. Boyle never came out of the back. Gail forgot where she was and laughed out loud at what happened to the bad guys.

She sobered as her father stopped the pickup in front of the store.

His face was grim when Gail stepped up into the cab. "How in tarnation did you manage to miss the bus?"

"I didn't know it would leave early."

"Did anyone else miss it?"

"No," she admitted. "I guess I took too long on the test, but I wanted to get the answers right. I left as soon as the bell rang."

"It's all-fired strange that you're the only one who missed the bus. You got to be more careful. You know how important every minute of daylight is to us right now."

Gail nodded. Her father rarely scolded her. He treated her like a responsible adult most of the time. She sat enclosed in a cloud of misery and fatigue all the way home.

"Get changed and help your mother with the milkin'," he said as they pulled into the cinder-covered driveway that separated the barn lot from the yard and their one-story white frame house. "I got to get back to the field."

The family didn't sit down for supper until almost eight o'clock. Gail's mother sent Bobby out back to the storm cellar to bring up the chicken she had fried at noon.

"Next spring we're getting a refrigerator," she said as she sliced the bread. "Then we won't have to keep anything but the cannin' and the apples outside in the cave."

Bobby heaped his plate high. "How do you like junior high, Gail?"

She opened her mouth to spew out all the hurts and disappointments, but she stopped herself when she saw how anxiously her parents waited for her answer. Instead she said, "You can't say after one day."

Her mother frowned. "What's wrong? Are you behind

Chapter Three

the town kids?"

Gail considered a moment. "Only in algebra and volleyball."

Her father shrugged this off. "You've always been good at arithmetic, and volleyball is just a game."

Bobby stopped chewing long enough to say, "Did you make any friends?"

Gail saw no reason to mention Red and face Bobby's teasing. "Sort of. Noreen Boyle helped me find a coupla classes and took me to the store to call. Mr. Boyle said he used to play ball with you, Dad."

He nodded. "He was a top-notch pitcher. He tried out for the Cardinals once. It's a shame how he's—uh—he's let his business go to pot since his wife died. She kept it runnin' all the time he was in the Army, but she died a couple years after the war ended."

Gail felt so sorry for motherless Noreen that tears of sympathy welled up.

Her mother didn't notice. "Didn't his older girl elope with a sailor last winter? I've heard this one runs around like she's eighteen. I don't think you should have much to do with her."

Gail took a bite of chicken to excuse herself from replying. She had no intention of avoiding the one girl who'd been nice to her.

"Now, Gail," her mother said, "don't give me that stubborn look. You're new, and the other kids will judge you by your friends."

Gail said nothing, but she thought, "And by the clothes you wear."

"Your mother's right," her father said. "You don't want to start off on the wrong foot. Make friends with some nice girls, like Harry Holt's granddaughter."

Knowing if she said one word, she'd say too many, Gail held her tongue.

Chapter Four

Gail was waiting by the road when the bus topped the long hill east of the house the next morning.

"Why did you go off without me last night?" she asked the young man driving as she boarded the bus.

He looked surprised. "Everybody there got a ride home." He turned his attention to the road.

Angry and embarrassed, she made her way to the back where Alice sat.

"Red and me asked him to wait," Alice said. "I'm really sorry."

Gail wanted to yell at everyone on the bus, but she swallowed her anger and talked to her friends about their first day until the bus pulled up to the school.

The doors were already open. Gail rushed in, got what she needed from her locker, and slipped into her seat in homeroom a minute or so after the three-minute warning bell rang.

Remembering that she wanted to look up the word Noreen had called the principal, Gail asked to borrow the dictionary on the teacher's desk.

Mrs. Ransler handed it to her with a smile as the last bell rang. The teacher's eyes lingered on Noreen's empty chair. "Good morning," she said to the class. "I'm glad to see how quickly some of you are getting into the spirit of learning. Gail started her day by looking up a word."

Knowing a teacher's praise hurt more than it helped with other students, Gail hoped they'd forgotten her name.

"What word are you learning, Gail?" Mrs. Ransler asked. "Maybe we can all add to our vocabulary today."

Gail remembered the English teacher's disapproval when she had declined to read her paper the day before. "Bastard," she said.

O.T. howled with laughter, and several others giggled. Mrs. Ransler hid her mouth with her roll book.

"Someone used it yesterday," Gail said. She found the word and skimmed the definitions. Quickly she read aloud the least offensive one: "It's a disagreeable person."

Mrs. Ransler smiled. "Did the person use the word correctly?"

"They sure did."

"He *surely* did," Mrs. Ransler said. She began to call the roll.

Chapter Four

Noreen strolled in just as the teacher called her name. Mrs. Ransler hesitated a moment before moving on to the next name.

The students spent homeroom reading three pages of school rules.

"I have one rule to add," Mrs. Ransler said. "Absolutely no slam books. I'll send anyone who carries or writes in one straight to the principal's office."

Gail was mystified. "What are slam books?" she asked O.T. as the bell rang.

"Notebooks with a kid's name at the top of each page. Kids pass them around and write nasty stuff under the names. And don't sign it."

"That's mean," Gail said, tucking the rules into her notebook.

O.T. and Noreen tossed theirs in the wastepaper basket.

The second day went well for Gail, and each day that week she felt more at ease. She began to learn other students' names and to raise her hand to answer teachers' questions. Her confidence grew as she saw she could hold her own everywhere except algebra and phys ed. Best of all, Veronica and her snobbish friends ignored Gail and everyone else who wasn't part of their clique.

Even so, Gail woke up early Saturday morning jubilant that the day marked the start of the three-day Labor Day weekend and the county fair. While her parents were still at the barn milking the cows, she baked biscuits to enter in

The Feedsack Dress

the 4-H cooking project competition. As soon as the biscuits were out of the oven, she rushed outside to shoo her two best pullets and her best rooster into a portable pen she'd hammered together out of scraps of lumber and chicken wire. She was entering them in the poultry competition.

Bobby hadn't been old enough to join 4-H last year, but he'd been a Missouri Nature Knight at school. For his fair entry, he'd spent a morning remounting the tree bark, leaves, and dried wild plants he'd collected during third grade. Their mother chose ten big, red, smooth tomatoes for the horticultural competition, and their father had a small bag of oats and ten ears of corn. As exhibitors, they wouldn't have to pay the admission fee.

When the Albrights parked in the field by the fairgrounds, Gail noticed that a lot of people, including farmers, were getting out of new cars. She envied them, but she knew her father wouldn't even think about a car until he'd paid off the mortgage.

"I should be working in the field instead of parking in one," he said as he lifted Gail's chickens out of the pickup.

"The fair is once a year," his wife reminded him.

He put his hand in a top pocket of his overalls. "I guess you kids want your allowance quarter and an extra quarter for the fair."

Bobby's face fell. "Only one quarter for the whole fair?"

"That's only one Ferris wheel ride and a couple bottles of pop," Gail protested.

Chapter Four

Her father grinned. "A dollar each then, but make it last. Let's get our stuff registered."

When Gail finished registering her entries, she went to the clothing section of the home economics tent to look for Alice. She was standing with two new friends near the racks filled with dresses made by 4-H'ers. Gail noticed that only two or three had been made from feedsacks.

"We'll ask Gail. She always knows stuff," Alice said. "Gail, how much prize money do we get for a blue ribbon?"

"That depends on how many come to the fair," Gail said. "The admission money goes for prizes. Last year we got ten cents a point."

"Even if my wool dress gets a blue ribbon, I can earn only ten points. Just a dollar for all that work," a girl in jeans and a feedsack blouse said.

"On your way to the cattle shed to see Red's calf, Gail?" Alice asked, nudging one of the other girls.

She giggled. "Let's all go. That's where the boys are."

When the girls approached the big tin-roofed, open-sided shed, about twenty boys and five girls in a large circle were trying to make their half-grown Hereford calves stand quietly. The three judges called out one sturdy calf at a time and ran expert hands over it to evaluate the animal's build and the quality of care it had received.

The other girls went into the shed, but Gail stayed to watch Red lead his calf into the center of the circle.

Although the Albrights raised dairy cattle, Gail knew

that Red's baby beef entry was a fine animal. Its white head was well shaped, and the curly, dark red hair on the stocky body gleamed with health. Not a speck of dirt marred the coat.

Bobby appeared at her elbow. "How come you're watchin' this? You said cattle judgin' is boring."

"I came over with Alice."

Bobby looked around. "She ain't here." He turned his attention to the ring. "Is that red-headed kid with the freckles your boyfriend?"

Gail glared at him. "Would you like to be strangled with your own tongue?"

"He's getting a blue. That's worth ten bucks and a chance for Junior Best of Breed. Maybe even Grand Champion."

"Hi, Gail!" Red called, leading his calf toward her as the contestants started back toward the shed. His smile expanded as he drew nearer.

"Hi." Gail tried to sound friendly but not girlfriendly. She wished Bobby would disappear.

"Meet Huckleberry, the new Grand Champion, I hope."

Bobby's eyes widened. "Gosh. Mr. Holt said he'd pay $350 for the junior winner this year. Dad said that's a hundred over market price."

Red sobered. "We sure could use the money. Jack, my brother, got a blue, too, but his calf ain't—isn't—as

Chapter Four

good as mine, and it's harder to handle. Come on back and I'll show you where we keep 'em."

Gail thought it only polite to go along.

A worried-looking redhead only slightly taller than Bobby stood waiting for them. "Red, I can't get Caribou to go back into the shed."

"I'll give you a hand," Gail offered. She gripped the rope halter with one hand and ran her other soothingly along the velvety neck of the nervous calf.

Caribou stepped forward and walked calmly through the crowded shed to the space where rectangular bales of yellow straw formed stall walls and provided the carpet for the animals' bedding.

Red beamed. "You got a way with cattle, Gail."

"Caribou likes girls," Jack said. He giggled. "So does Red."

Red's face turned the color of his hair.

"We've got to meet our folks in the bleachers for lunch," Gail said, turning to hide her own face. "See ya later." She took off and kept well ahead of her little brother as they charged past the exhibition tents and up the midway.

They found their parents about halfway up the bleachers. Nothing was happening on the stage or the oval track, but people had come early to socialize.

"Sure would be nice to be in the shade like those folks in the grandstand," Bobby said as he held out his tin cup for lemonade from the thermos jug his father usually carried

The Feedsack Dress

with him to the field.

"If you can play all day in the sun, I reckon the free seats won't kill you," his father said, waving a drumstick at his son. "But if you want to spend your money for a seat in the shade, go ahead."

"I ain't that stupid." Bobby held the cold cup to his forehead.

By the time the harness races started, everyone was fanning with cardboard fans handed out by a funeral parlor.

Gail couldn't take her eyes off the elegant trotters and pacers with their glistening coats, braided tails, and polished leather harnesses. They looked like a different species from the plodding workhorses that Gail drove hitched to the hay wagon. She imagined riding in a light two-wheeled cart and keeping a trotter going at full speed without breaking into a disqualifying gallop.

When only the final heats of each of the three-heat races remained, the announcer bellowed into his microphone, "And now, ladies and gentlemen, you're about to see a display of speed unmatched on any race track—thank goodness. Boys, bring out your Missouri mules!"

The crowd laughed as a group of men and boys pulled and pushed four mules from the infield onto the track. It took them five minutes to get the strong-willed animals into an uneven starting line.

An unsaddled white mule remained riderless until the starter fired his pistol. But at the sound of the shot, the rider

Chapter Four

sprang onto his back with a loud whoop and the mule trotted down the track.

"It's Red!" Gail gasped, grabbing Bobby's arm.

Red's white mule took the lead as one gray mule galloped in the wrong direction, another stood stock still, and the fourth crowhopped at the starting line.

Red's mule saw the open gate into the infield and trotted through it. Red pulled on the reins, yelled, and dug his heels into the mule's sides. It bent its head for a bite of grass. Spectators rushed to help, but their shouts and slaps to the mule's rump did no good.

The bucker had made slight headway, and the rider headed the wrong way managed to turn his mount around and proceed at a fast walk. The fourth mule remained rooted to the starting line.

Red's mule lifted its head to watch the two mules going around the track. It whirled around to follow, almost throwing him off. As he clung to the mane, his mule loped after the leaders, braying to them all the while.

"Ride him, Red!" the announcer shouted, and the crowd cheered.

When Red caught up with the other two mules in the homestretch, his steed slowed to a rough trot just behind the bucker. The mule on the inside rail leapt forward, losing his surprised rider, and galloped over to the outer rail. There it stood, staring at the people in the bleachers.

Ten feet from the finish line, the bucker resumed his

crowhopping. Red's mule turned to watch the other animal head back up the homestretch. Face grim, Red fought to turn his mule back toward the finish line. The mule stood his ground. After a few seconds, Red let the reins go loose and sat absolutely still. Then he started to whistle "Yankee Doodle" and pull back on the reins.

Inch by inch the white mule backed over the finish line.

"White Lightning wins by a tail," the announcer boomed.

"That's Gail's boyfriend," Bobby yelled as the crowd clapped and hooted.

Gail concealed her burning face behind her fan, but she hoped Bobby was right.

Chapter Five

In spite of the lingering heat, the Albrights finished the milking, water pumping, and egg gathering in record time that evening. By 7:30 they had returned to the fairgrounds.

The whole family went to the exhibition tent to water and feed Gail's chickens.

"I expect I'll just get a red ribbon," Gail said as she looked at the competition.

"Your pullets look pretty good to me," Red said, coming up behind her.

Her father slapped Red on the back. "Howdy, cowboy. Nice job with your mule."

"You sure were funny," Bobby said.

Red cleared his throat. "Gail, I thought it might be fun to go watch people try to dunk our principal at the Rotary Club's booth."

"You bet! He could stand a good soaking."

Her mother smiled. "Your principal must be a good sport if he's taking a turn on the dunking stool. Go ahead, Gail. Come on up to the bleachers when you're ready."

"I'll go with Gail," Bobby said.

His mother put her hand on his shoulder. "Let's go see if the judges have put the ribbons on the Nature Knight collections instead."

Gail and Red hurried out of the tent and down the carnival midway past the merry-go-round, the Ferris wheel, the tilt-a-whirl, games of skill and chance, and the Oliver Tractor exhibit, her father's favorite hangout.

About fifty students stood in front of the Rotary Club's booth, where the principal sat on a board suspended over a head-high tank of water. He wore an old-fashioned long-legged black bathing suit, a derby hat too small for his head, and the expression of a man waiting for the dentist.

Phil, the star athlete who hung around Veronica, was juggling three baseballs. "This one has Oliver T. Addison written on it."

Gail gulped. The principal had the same name as O.T. She tried to remember what nasty things she'd said in front of O.T. about the man who must be his father.

"Come on, muscle man," O.T. yelled. "He's only got two minutes left on his shift."

Flexing his muscles, Phil wound up and hurled a ball at the saucer-sized target that would release the seat and

Chapter Five

dump the principal in the water. He missed by an inch. His second ball nicked the saucer's edge. His third ball missed by a hair.

Gail let her desire to dunk the principal drown out the inner voice of better judgment. "How much is it, mister?"

"Three throws for a quarter."

"Here's my quarter," Gail said. Heart pounding, she picked up a baseball from a box. Unlike a volleyball, it felt at home in her hand. She eyed the target. It didn't look all that hard to hit for someone who had thrown hundreds of rocks at fence posts, but Mr. Addison's bathing suit was dry.

Red leaned close. "You got to hit it dead center."

The kids were yelling encouragement and jokes about throwing eggs, but she ignored them. Taking a deep breath, she wound up as if she were pitching to Stan the Man Musial in the ninth.

Her pitch brushed the edge of the target, and Mr. Addison smiled.

Gail gritted her teeth and threw as hard as she could.

His smile became a smirk as her second throw missed the target by half a foot. Several of the students watching groaned, and others laughed and hooted.

Gail set her jaw and pretended she was throwing at a fence post. Her third pitch whacked against the target, and a split second later the principal dropped into the tank.

"Got him!" Gail said under her breath. No moment had ever seemed sweeter.

The Feedsack Dress

The students whooped and applauded as he wiped water from his eyes with one hand and felt for the ladder with the other.

Gail struggled to hide her exultation as classmates who'd never spoken to her congratulated her, but her triumph evaporated as Veronica whispered something to Phil and they both laughed.

Gail nudged Red toward an open space. "Let's go."

"You got a good arm," he said as they broke through the crowd.

"I really wanted to dunk that—uh—you know."

"That bastard?" He chuckled. "Yeah, I looked it up, too."

"I didn't tell anyone that was who I meant."

"It wasn't too hard to guess. How 'bout we take a look at the midway?"

They walked and watched people trying to win stuffed animals and cheap doodads by flipping pennies on a big board with small squares, throwing baseballs at bottles, shooting toy guns at a moving line of little yellow wooden ducks, tossing rings over canning jars, and netting fake fish.

Gail knew that in the movies the boy always stopped and tried to win a prize for the girl, but Red didn't do that. And he walked just far enough away from her that they never accidentally touched. He'd asked her to come with him, but maybe she just happened to be the first person he saw that he knew.

Chapter Five

Talking on the bus had been easy and natural. Now Gail didn't know what to say. Apparently he didn't either. To break the silence, she asked him about his calf.

Red gave her a history of what he'd fed Huckleberry from his birth. As they reached the Ferris wheel, he said, "I'll walk you up to the bleachers, if you're ready to go. I got to go back to the barn to get the calves settled down."

Disappointed that he hadn't suggested a ride on the Ferris wheel, Gail nodded and turned to walk toward the bleachers.

When they reached the free seats, Alice called and waved at them.

"See ya tomorrow," Red said. He practically ran back into the shadows.

The bleachers didn't have aisles, but Gail worked her way up the splintery boards to where Alice and several other girls watched the stage show. The owner of Craigsburg's new, and only, radio station introduced a square dance group from Hannibal. A country music band who played on Station WHO in Des Moines, the big station most people listened to, followed. The show ended with eight baton twirlers performing on the track in front of the grandstand. The record providing the music had to be restarted twice before they got into their routine.

When Alice and the other girls headed for the midway, Gail trailed along pretending to be interested in their talk of clothes and hair-dos and high school football players. She nodded and wondered if she should have offered to go to the barn with Red. Just as she found the courage to suggest the girls all go by the cattle barn, Bobby came to tell her it was time to go home.

Walking toward the pickup, Gail reflected that solving algebra problems was easier than figuring out boys.

Chapter Six

Sunday afternoon Red and his pal Pete were standing by the Ferris wheel as Gail and Alice got off. It seemed natural for the four of them to walk together through the carnival and then the merchants' tents with their displays of farm machinery, electrical appliances, tires, and cars. The four signed up for all the prizes, from a sack of feed corn to a red convertible. Finally they went to the bleachers to watch the last two harness races. Everyone took it for granted that Red would sit next to Gail.

Sunday evening the four met "accidentally" at the rifle-shot booth and walked to the tents to see what ribbons the girls had received. Alice blushed at the sight of a blue first-place ribbon on her dress. Gail sighed at the red second-place ribbon on her biscuits, but she felt better when she saw a blue ribbon on her chickens' cage.

When they reached the cattle barn, Red proudly displayed Huckleberry's big purple Best of Breed ribbon. While he and Gail talked about how he would compete with the best animals of other breeds and weights for Grand Champion Monday night, Alice and Pete slipped away.

"Pete's kinda sweet on Alice," Red said when he missed them. He picked up a curry brush. "Want to help me brush Huckleberry? He loves it."

Gail wished he would say he was sweet on her. She hoped that's what an invitation to help with Huckleberry meant.

Monday morning—Labor Day—Gail offered to help clean two frying chickens, a chore she detested.

The first step was to catch the prey. Her mother pointed out the ones she wanted, and Gail and Bobbie cornered them between the garden fence and the chicken house.

Her mother held the first on the old stump that served as a chopping block. She raised her hatchet in her free hand, chopped off the head with one whack, and tossed the body several feet away so that it would not splatter blood on her as it thrashed around.

She turned to Gail with a smile. "In a hurry to get to the fair for some reason?"

Gail felt herself go pink. "Sorta." She handed her mother the second chicken, picked up the dead one by its twitching legs, and submerged it in a bucket of hot water.

Chapter Six

She held her breath to avoid the stench of wet chicken feathers. When she was sure the chicken was completely soaked, she lifted it out and started pulling out the feathers. She held it as far away from her as she could. "Even manure doesn't smell as bad as wet feathers. I guess I'm finally getting tired of fried chicken. We've had it 'most every day for weeks."

Her mother chopped and tossed. "Got to eat things when they're ready. This winter you'll be gripin' that we never have fried chicken—only old bakin' hens."

The moment the chicken stopped moving, Mrs. Albright picked it up and dunked it in the bucket. "Gail, I think you should wear your mornin' glory dress today. I love the way it matches your eyes."

Gail threw a handful of feathers into an old bushel basket. She thought about mentioning how the town kids made fun of feedsack dresses, but she knew that would hurt her mother's feelings.

"Honey, don't you like that dress?"

Gail concentrated on plucking feathers. "I was just thinking that I ought to save it for school."

"That's all right. I'll do the wash tomorrow."

Gail gave up.

From then on the day went wrong. When they reached the fair that afternoon, Red was so busy fussing over Huckleberry that he paid little attention to Gail. She went to the bleachers with Alice and two girls who said little and giggled a lot. In the middle of the harness races, the sky darkened and a wall of rain moved across the fields toward them. Everyone ran for shelter.

Gail ended up in the John Deere tent. Her parents had beat her there, and her father stood gazing wistfully at a tractor.

Gail's mother sighed. "I wish he'd look that way at a car. We really need something besides that old pickup. But then you can't take pigs to market in a car."

The rain soon moved on by, but it left the fairgrounds muddy and slippery. Gail and Bobby didn't object when their parents suggested they go on home.

When they'd finished the chores and had supper, Gail put her feedsack dress back on but wore her old shoes for the muddy midway.

Alice's family pulled into the fairgrounds right behind the Albrights, and the two girls headed toward the barn.

They found Red with Huckleberry, but his usual wide grin was missing.

"What's wrong?" Gail asked.

He looked away. "It's so messy on that track in front of the grandstand that Huck is goin' to be filthy when the judges look at him."

"Maybe you can clean him up while the announcer is talking at the end of the Grand Parade."

He still didn't look at her. "Maybe."

Gail couldn't figure out why he was so upset. After all,

Chapter Six

every finalist faced the same problem. "You want to win pretty bad, don't you?"

Running the curry brush down Huck's side, Red said, "I need to win." He turned and picked up another curry brush.

Pete, leading his calf toward the shed's opening, paused a moment. "Your dad asked me to tell you the pigs got out. He and Jack were out roundin' them up when we drove by."

"Dang!" Red threw down a brush. "I'll bet old Muddauber dug his way under the fence and led the whole bunch to his favorite mudhole down in the creek. It'll take hours to get them in. I better find somebody else to lead Caribou in the Grand Parade." He looked around and waved at someone a few stalls down. "'Scuse me, Gail." He handed her the curry brush before walking away.

Caribou bawled as if he, too, was worried about his missing owner. Gail talked to the calf as she did to nervous dairy cows and ran the curry brush down his side. The calf was looking at her with his soulful brown eyes when Red returned.

"They just gave the order to line up, and I can't find anybody."

He looked so miserable that Gail blurted, "I could do it. At least get him in line. Maybe your folks will get here before we go onto the track anyway."

Red hesitated. "He's a pretty strong calf, and he's not as calm as Huck. You sure you can handle him?"

Gail wasn't sure at all, but she couldn't back out now.

The Feedsack Dress

"I think so, and there's nobody else."

"That's great, Gail. Thanks a lot. I'll stay as close to you as I can."

Caribou seemed quite content to have Gail by his side. She kept one hand on the halter rope and the other on the calf's neck as Red and Huckleberry led the way out of the barn to where the Herefords were lining up.

Walking through the muddy field, she gave thanks that she'd worn her old shoes. She envied the kids showing sheep. Instead of wading through the muck, they had loaded their animals onto a big open-bed Holt's Feed truck and were kneeling beside them.

When the signal came to walk to the track, the skittish Black Angus moved out first. The calmer Herefords followed, with Red and Huckleberry, as Best of Breed, in the lead. Gail and Caribou brought up the end of the Hereford line, far away from any help from Red.

Caribou held back as they moved single file onto the lighted track in front of the grandstand. He was the last of dozens of animals, most of them handled by young owners. As each paraded past the grandstand and turned to form a semicircle, feedstore owner Harry Holt announced the owner's and the animal's name over the loudspeaker.

"There go the feedsacks," Veronica said as Gail walked past the Holt box.

Gail stared straight ahead at the tail of the calf in front of her. She didn't even look up when she heard

Chapter Six

someone yell and struggle to pull an Angus calf back in line. The audience laughed, and some boys in the crowd hooted.

"And last of this fine group, Jack Royce with Caribou," Mr. Holt said. "Oops! 'Scuse me, folks! That's Miss Gail Albright standing in for Jack."

Gail hadn't thought her name would be announced. Now everyone knew who the girl in the feedsack dress was. Probably all the people sitting in the grandstand would think her family was poor.

Caribou jumped to one side, reminding Gail she had other things to worry about. So much mud clumped on her shoes that it was hard to walk, but she and Caribou finally took their place at the end of the semicircle. She relaxed as Red and four others led their Best of Breed animals into the center of the semicircle for the final judging to name the Grand Champion.

Caribou mooed to his pal Huck.

Gail tightened her grip on the halter just as Caribou lunged forward. She jerked on the halter, but the eight-hundred-pound yearling pulled away. She hung on and tried to pull him back, but he dragged her toward the center of the ring. She fell on one knee, barely keeping her hold on the halter. Caribou stopped and looked at her as though he was surprised to see her there. The audience laughed as she struggled to her feet.

Caribou lunged forward again, forcing Gail to slip and slide toward the judges.

"Red, help me!"

He didn't move. "Pinch his nose," he yelled.

Caribou changed course to take a closer look at the noisy grandstand. Gail tried to dig in her heels to hold him. For a second Caribou pulled her over the wet track as though she were on skis. Then her feet slipped and she sat down hard.

The fall didn't hurt. Seeing Veronica laughing hysterically did.

Chapter Seven

One of the judges rushed to help Gail to her feet. She waved him back with assurances that she hadn't been hurt.

"That's real spirit for you," Mr. Holt said to the crowd. "Let's give the young lady a hand."

Smiling weakly, Gail waved to acknowledge the applause. Furious that Red had let her become Veronica's entertainment, she wanted to drop Caribou's halter and march off, but her pride and Mr. Holt's praise kept her there.

Taking a firm grip on the calf's halter and nose, she coaxed it back to its place at the end of the line. She expressed her anger by not cheering when the judges declared Huckleberry Grand Champion.

While Red and Huckleberry posed for the *Craigsburg*

The Feedsack Dress

Monitor's photographer, Gail led a subdued Caribou back to the barn, tied him in his stall, and went to the spigot to wash mud off her hands, arms, legs, and face.

Alice came to help remove the mud caked on the back of the dress.

Gail picked flecks off the front. "One good thing—I've ruined this darn feedsack dress. Let's get out of here before Red comes back. I'm so mad at him I can't see straight."

At the entrance to the barn, they ran into Red. Gail glared at him in a way that would have made Ratter yelp and run to hide out in the cornfield.

Red ignored the shouts of congratulations coming at him from all sides. "Gosh, I'm sorry, Gail. But I couldn't let go of Huckleberry and risk his acting up and losing Grand Champion."

Gail wondered how she could have thought he liked her, or that she liked him. "Nothing is so important to you as winning, is it? That's all you've been thinking about the whole fair."

She ran out of the tent to the Albrights' pickup to avoid facing anyone.

Her mother was waiting for her. "Let's see the dress." She inspected it in the dim light. "I don't know if I can get this clean, but I'll sure try. What were you thinking to go out there in that mud? I know you like that Royce boy, but you should've realized you couldn't handle that calf. You've got to stop rushin' into things."

Chapter Seven

* * *

By the time Gail stepped on the school bus the next morning, she'd remembered that she had volunteered to take Caribou because she wanted to impress Red. She owned part of the blame for her humiliation. Ready to accept Red's apology, she smiled as she started toward the back of the bus.

One of the high school boys sitting up front grinned at her. "Hey, Gail, how come you sat down on the job last night?"

Others chimed in.

"Are mud baths really good for the skin?"

"I've heard of waterskiing, but that's the first time I ever saw mudskiing."

Embarrassed by the teasing, Gail curved her lips into a nervous smile. She looked away from Red as she passed him, and he made no effort to speak to her on the bus or at school.

From the comments in the halls, everyone at Craigsburg Junior High had seen the Grand Parade. And everyone made the same bad jokes she'd heard on the bus.

Even Phil, coming into homeroom with Veronica, grinned at Gail. "Hey there, cowgirl. You sure can throw a ball, but you need to work on your bulldogging."

He'd never even spoken to Gail before. Well aware he was the best looking boy in the class, she mumbled, "I guess I'm better with chickens than cattle."

O.T. snickered. "You sure laid an egg last night."

Mrs. Ransler frowned at him as she handed out sign-up forms for extracurricular activities. Gail ignored the ones after school and skimmed those at noon: Personal Grooming, Intramural Sports, Knitting, and Special Reading. None appealed to her.

She read the after-school list: Glee Club, Art Club, Little Theater, School Patrol, Stamp Club, Chess Club, and Great American Novels.

She sighed and whispered, "All the good stuff is after the bus leaves."

O.T. tapped his pencil on Intramural Sports. "Anybody who can throw a baseball the way you do should like intramurals."

"Not volleyball." Gail checked to see that Mrs. Ransler was still occupied at the other side of the room. "What's this Special Reading thing?"

Noreen looked up from a photo spread in *Life*. "That's for the dummies."

Mrs. Ransler came toward them. "Do you have a question over here?"

O.T. and Noreen studied their forms.

Gail met the teacher's eyes. "Extracurricular means not required, doesn't it?"

The teacher looked toward the back of the room. "Every student has to sign up for one extracurricular activity." She moved toward a noisy group in the back row.

"Check intramurals," Noreen whispered without raising her head. "You don't have to play. You can be a sub."

Gail took the advice.

Chapter Seven

* * *

By last period, Gail's face ached from the fake smiles she'd put on in response to the teasing about her fall in the mud. Her only real smile had come when the girls in the Jail cheered her for dunking the principal.

Walking into social studies, she congratulated herself for surviving the day without losing her temper enough to say something she'd regret.

Mrs. Ransler opened class by announcing a surprise. The owner of the radio station was considering having students from the junior and senior high schools write and broadcast weekly programs. He had asked her to choose five students to present a half-hour program on citizenship as a trial run.

"To be absolutely fair, I've chosen the students with the highest scores on the test I gave you the first day of school."

Gail remembered that test all too well. She'd spent so much time on it she'd missed the bus.

"Those students are Veronica Holt, Arthur Stiles, Ralph Toffani, and Noreen Boyle."

A little surprised but pleased that Noreen had done so well, Gail scribbled "congrats" on her notebook and showed it to her classmate.

O.T.'s hand shot up. "That's only four."

Mrs. Ransler smiled at the class. "Can you guess who had the top score?"

"It had to be Phil," Veronica said, turning to smile at him.

Mrs. Ransler shook her head no. She shook it no three more times. "The top score, an almost perfect paper, was made by a new student—Gail Albright."

Gail barely stifled a victory whoop. She glanced at Veronica and took pleasure in the shock on the blonde girl's face.

O.T. poked Gail with his elbow. "Great going."

Mrs. Ransler waited for the murmurs of surprise to run their course. "Those five students, three of whom happen to be in my homeroom and this class, will meet in my office during homeroom tomorrow to plan their work."

When the bell releasing the class rang, Gail hurried to her locker and then outside. Afraid the other junior high kids on her bus would think she was bragging, she waited until sliding into the seat beside Alice to share the good news.

Before Gail could say anything to Alice, Red paused at her seat. "Congratulations."

Gail turned sideways to avoid looking at him. "Thanks. I won't get any money for being on the radio, but I'll enjoy it anyway."

But she didn't enjoy the ride home. She ached to share her triumph with Red, and now, thanks to her quick temper and tongue, she couldn't.

Even sharing the good news with her parents didn't take away the sense of loss.

To make matters worse, her mother triumphantly brought out another surprise, the freshly washed and ironed

Chapter Seven

feedsack dress. Gail almost blurted out how much she hated it, how wearing it labeled her a poor hick, but looking at her mother's proud, tired face, she just couldn't say it.

The next morning she put on the feedsack dress, determined to get wearing it over with for the week.

When the bus came, she made a point of not looking at the seat where Red usually sat. Instead she talked to Alice about what to demonstrate in speech class the next Monday. Both had done demonstrations in 4-H, but neither one had any good ideas.

"We're a little late," the driver warned as the bus pulled up in front of the junior high. "You kids better not lollygag on your way to class."

Gail hurried through empty halls to her locker, tossed her lunch inside, grabbed her books, and ran into homeroom just as the last bell rang. Dropping her books on the arm of her chair, she flung herself into it—and heard the unmistakable crack of an eggshell.

Chapter Eight

Jumping out of her chair, Gail stared at the back of her dress in disbelief.

Mrs. Ransler, standing on the other side of the room, regarded her with surprise. "What's wrong, Gail?"

Choking with laughter, O.T. squeaked out, "I think she's laid an egg."

The giggles and laughs erupting around the classroom reminded Gail of all the humiliation and hurt she'd faced in the last few days. Grabbing O.T. by his ears, she jerked him up from his chair, pulled him a step to the left, and shoved him down on the broken egg.

Mrs. Ransler placed a restraining hand on Gail's shoulder. "That's enough! What on earth is going on?"

Noreen spoke from the door: "Would you like for me to go with Gail to help clean the egg off her dress?"

The teacher glanced down at Gail's dress, and

comprehension dawned on her face. "Yes, of course. Thank you, Noreen."

"Who's going to help *me*?" O.T. said, standing up and trying to wipe the egg off his jeans with a white handkerchief.

Mrs. Ransler sighed. "I wish I knew, O.T., I really do."

Gail followed Noreen into the girls' restroom. Anger had drained Gail's strength, and she wanted to cry with disappointment that O.T. had played such a mean trick on her.

Noreen turned on a faucet. "You've got quite a temper. I would never have guessed you'd explode that way."

"Me neither," Gail said. "I guess it's been buildin'—building—up. That egg was the last straw." Gail thought how ridiculous it was to call an egg a straw, and she'd said "me neither." She'd have to be more careful what she said and how she said it or Mrs. Ransler might decide she sounded too much like a hillbilly to be on the radio.

Noreen grabbed a roll of toilet paper from a stall. "Aw, you take those jerks too seriously. Besides, if they see they're getting to you, they'll just get worse. The best thing to do is ignore 'em." She poured some water from her cupped hand onto the back of Gail's dress, and began to rub the dress gently. "You got some sun coming up in your morning glories."

Gail managed a half-hearted smile. "Something ghastly happens every time I wear this damn feedsack dress. I hate it."

Noreen dampened more tissue. "It's a pretty dress."

Gail pushed the compliment aside. She wanted sympathy. "You don't know what it's like to have people talk about you for wearing a feedsack."

"That I don't," Noreen said, and her voice had turned cold. "That's as clean as I can get it. I don't know how to take out stains."

Not knowing what she'd said to offend Noreen, Gail plunged ahead. "Taking out stains isn't so hard if you've got the right stuff. Hey! You've just given me an idea of what I can demonstrate in my speech class." She grinned feebly. "At least I got something out of this."

Noreen moved toward the door. "That's the best I can do."

Gail trailed behind, wondering what she had said or done to upset her classmate.

O.T. was not in his seat, and every student was absorbed in a textbook when the girls returned to homeroom.

Mrs. Ransler intercepted Gail at the door. "Take your books and go to Mr. Addison's office, please. He wants to speak to you."

Dread flooded through Gail. "You—you told him what happened?"

"Not exactly. He came by as I was talking to O.T. in the hall and took him on down to the office."

Gathering up her books, Gail moved toward the

Chapter Eight

door.

Mrs. Ransler followed her into the hall. "Gail, whatever Mr. Addison has to say, hold your temper. You're too smart to lose self-control that way."

Gail's cheeks flamed. "I won't pop off like that again." Even as she said it, she wondered if she could keep her word. She wasn't used to such anger boiling up, and she didn't know how to handle it.

The bell rang for the first-period class as Gail stepped into the school office. A woman stood behind the high counter that separated the principal and his staff from the students and teachers. Not knowing what to do and intimidated by her surroundings, Gail waited until the woman had filled out a tardy slip for a boy.

She reached for her pad again. "And your excuse for being late?"

"I'm—I'm not late. I came to see Mr. Addison."

"He's busy right now." She turned to answer the phone.

When the woman finally hung up, Gail cleared her throat. "Should I wait or go on to class until he asks for me again?"

"What's your name, dear?"

"Gail Albright."

"Heavens, child! Why didn't you tell me?" The woman was half scolding, half laughing. "He's waiting for you." She opened the half door in the restraining wall for Gail and then the regular door to the principal's office. "This is Gail

Albright," she announced.

He looked up from a pile of papers. "I know who she is. Sit down, young lady."

Gail sat in the straight-backed chair in front of his desk.

He took a dark blue suit jacket off the back of his chair and drew it on as though donning a judge's robe.

A movement in a dark corner of the office caught her attention. O.T. was standing there staring at the floor.

"Please explain your behavior this morning," the principal said.

"My behavior?" Surprised to be put on the defensive, she glanced at O.T., but he didn't look up. She decided to get right to the point. "Okay. O.T. put an egg in my chair and I sat on it, so I put O.T. in my chair so he could have the same opportunity."

The principal frowned. "O.T. swears he did not put the egg there. But that is beside the point. I am the only one in this school who administers corporal punishment."

Gail's heart almost stopped. Was he going to paddle her?

He dabbed his forehead with a handkerchief. "Not even the teachers are allowed to touch a student. Your display of temper was not only unladylike and unjustified but a flagrant violation of school rules. First, I want you to apologize to O.T. for both your false accusation and your violence to his person."

Relief washed over Gail. He didn't mean to use a

Chapter Eight

paddle. She turned to O.T.

"Did you put that egg in my chair?"

He stepped toward her. "No! Honest, Gail, I didn't do it!"

She believed him, but that didn't get him off the hook. "But you knew it was there."

"Well, gee, sure, but—"

"And you didn't warn me."

"No, but Jumpin' Jehosophat, I didn't think you'd really sit on it. You rushed in so fast—"

"But you could have kept me from sitting on it, and you sure laughed hard enough when I did." Gail turned to Mr. Addison. "I can't honestly say I'm sorry. O.T. was an accomplice, sort of. He had it coming to him."

The principal's face went paper white. "Your attitude is reprehensible, and your action was a totally undisciplined flouting of authority. It must and shall be punished." He rose and turned his back to them, staring out the window.

O.T. had gone white, too. "Apologize," he mouthed to Gail in the instant before his father faced them again.

"O.T., go to class."

Gail's anger at the boy evaporated as she pitied him for having such a mean father. "I'm sorry, O.T.," she said with complete sincerity.

The principal nodded in approval. "That's better."

"I didn't mean—" Gail began, but O.T., just outside the door, held up his hands in mock prayer a moment before rushing away. He had understood her meaning. Gail stopped herself. She'd already waded in over her head. "Never mind."

The principal studied her face. "Saying you're sorry here isn't enough. You will make a public apology to O.T. tomorrow morning in the homeroom, and you will apologize to all the homeroom for your irresponsible and disruptive behavior."

Gail needed a dictionary to find out what disruptive meant, but it didn't sound good. She recognized that she deserved a reprimand, but so did someone else. Mr. Addison didn't care about that. Knowing she was throwing fuel on the fire but too angry to care, she said, "I'll be glad to apologize in homeroom, right after whoever put that egg in my chair apologizes to me."

He threw up his hands. "You will not dictate conditions, young lady. I will deal with the prankster as I see fit, not as you wish."

Gail would have bet her chicken money no one else would be punished. She pressed her lips together to hold back the words.

"What do you have to say?"

Gail considered giving in, but she'd never been good at that. "I've said what I have to say."

"I'd meant to let you off," he almost shouted, "but you leave me no alternative. Until you choose to make a public apology, you will spend half an hour in detention after school each day."

Chapter Eight

Gail was stunned. For the first time she thought of her parents' reaction to what she'd done. "I can't stay after school! I have to catch the bus!"

He rubbed his forehead again. "Yes, of course, the bus." He turned to look out the window again. After half a minute he said, "You will spend your lunch hour alone in your chair in your homeroom until you apologize."

Gail nodded and did her best to hide her relief. That wasn't much worse than sitting in the Jail, and she would be able to do her homework from her morning classes rather than working on it at home.

He rubbed his forehead again. "Go on to class. I'll tell Mrs. Ransler to notify me when you apologize." He cleared his throat as she rose. "I want to make it clear that this punishment has nothing to do with your —uh—skill with a baseball or with my son's involvement in the incident."

Gail smiled as she remembered him sputtering in the water. The fact that he'd mentioned it made her suspect it galled him. She let her smile widen as she walked out.

By the time Gail had received an excuse to enter speech class, first period was almost over. Coming down the hall, she heard Veronica's voice and remembered that this was the first day of demonstrations. Gail stopped just outside the door so her entrance would not be "irresponsible and disruptive behavior."

"And that," Veronica said, "is how you make egg custard."

Chapter Nine

"So that's where the egg came from," Gail said to herself. She stepped through the door at the back of the classroom and handed her excuse to Miss Harlan.

The teacher motioned for Gail to take her seat. "Are there any questions for Veronica?"

The class went dead quiet as Gail walked to her front-row chair.

Veronica gathered up her utensils, placing everything except the custard dish in a picnic basket. "Linda will take this to bake in home ec next period."

Miss Harlan walked to the front of the room. "Who would like to comment on the demonstration?"

No one spoke.

The teacher waited and waited. "Linda, what did you think of the way Veronica handled being short one

Chapter Nine

egg?"

Linda, a skinny, long-haired brunette who followed Veronica around like a puppy, stared at the floor and shrugged.

Students shuffled their feet and cleared their throats. Miss Harlan raised a questioning eyebrow. Gail felt eyes on her, but no one said anything. The teacher glanced at the excuse in her hand. "Gail, did you break Veronica's egg?"

Gail felt sure she had, but she wanted Veronica to admit it. "Ask her."

Veronica's cheeks turned pink. "I just—my mother was short of eggs this morning."

The bell rang, and the students gathered their books in slow motion with their eyes on the front of the room.

Gail guessed they were waiting for her to accuse Veronica of putting the missing egg in the chair, but having accused O.T. wrongly, Gail didn't dare be wrong again. Someone else could have taken the egg, though probably not without Veronica knowing it. Gail picked up her books and hurried out the door toward English class.

All through English and algebra Gail kept asking herself why Veronica or anyone else would play such a mean, pointless joke.

At noon Gail went to her locker to get her lunch and drop off everything but her algebra book.

Alice came up to her. "Ready to go to Jail?"

"I can't. I've got a private cell today. I'll tell you about it on the bus."

Alice followed her to Mrs. Ransler's room. "I don't get it."

Gail didn't speak until the hall cleared. "I'm on detention. I have to spend lunch hour alone in my homeroom. Go on to the Jail before you get in trouble."

When Gail came into the room, Mrs. Ransler put down a blackboard eraser and picked up her purse from her desk. "Gail, I hope you understand that what you did this morning was wrong, not to mention foolish. You should have left it to me to punish O.T. for putting that egg in your chair."

"He said he didn't do it, and I believe him."

The teacher studied her a moment. "And did Mr. Addison believe him?"

"Of course. He would know if his son was fibbing."

"If his son *were* fibbing. It's subjunctive. Then you don't blame O.T.?"

Two hours ago Gail had. Now she'd cooled down. "Some. He could've stopped me, so he's partly responsible. He didn't get anything he didn't deserve."

"Gail, you have no right to dispense justice." She sighed. "Why did you bring this detention on yourself by refusing to apologize in homeroom?"

Gail struggled for the words to express her feeling of being treated unfairly. "I don't see why I should apologize to the kids who were nasty to me. It's like saying, 'Excuse me for living.'"

Mrs. Ransler smiled. "I understand your point of view,

Chapter Nine

but it's shortsighted. Do you know who put the egg in your chair?"

"Not for absolute sure, and I don't know why either."

"Don't dwell on it, Gail. You've made a good start here, and trying to pay someone back will only ruin that." She touched Gail on the shoulder and left.

After Gail ate her bologna sandwich and apple, she worked on her algebra for twenty minutes. She told herself it was great to have the time and quiet to do her homework, but she missed relaxing with Alice and the other regulars in the Jail. She also had time to wonder about what her folks would say. She was so glad when the bell rang that she forgot her dread of phys ed.

Margie, a wiry little ball of energy with the quick temper and movements of a banty hen, had the pull-out metal basket next to Gail's. She already had hung up her skirt and blouse and was putting on her gym shorts.

"What happened in ol' Addison's office this morning? Did he give O.T. hell?"

"No." Gail didn't want to talk about it. She was relieved to slip out of her dress. The spot where she'd sat on the egg looked wrinkled but not stained.

Several girls gathered around her. One of the Jail regulars asked, "Why weren't you in the lunchroom today?"

Gail took a deep breath. She had nothing to be ashamed of, she reminded herself as she pulled on her white, short-sleeved gym blouse. "I'm on detention at noon."

"For how long?"

"I don't know." Gail couldn't stop herself. "Mr. Addison said I'm on detention until I apologize to the class, and I said I won't until whoever put the egg in my chair apologizes to me."

"Then you'll be on detention all year," Noreen said. She was already in her gym clothes. "If you're smart, you'll say you're sorry and get the whole thing over with."

"I sure would," Margie agreed. "I think it's unfair when you-know-who started it. Of course, when your grandfather is on the school board—"

Linda stuck her head around a wall of gym baskets. "Just shut up! If Shabby Abby hadn't galloped in there like a clumsy cow, everything would have been fine!"

Gail's mouth dropped open and her right hand curled into a fist.

Noreen pushed Gail and Margie toward the door of the locker room. "Let's go. We need to get in some practice before class starts if we're going to win the tournament this year."

Knowing Noreen was right to avoid trouble, Gail went. She expected to let her anger out by calling Linda and Veronica names as soon as they were in the gym.

Instead Noreen hustled her to the volleyball net. "You're taller than most of the girls. We need you to hit spikes. Margie, set some up for us."

Noreen jumped straight in the air to spike the first

Chapter Nine

ball Margie tapped over the net.

"Okay, Gail, now you do it."

Gail tried three times, and three times she hit the ball into the net.

"Concentrate," Noreen said. "You can do this."

Pushing "Shabby Abby" to the back of her mind to be brought out again for some bedtime tears, Gail tried to put her anger into hitting the ball. She finally hit two anemic spikes over the net. Margie returned both.

Hard as Gail tried during the exercises and games that day, the balls bounced off her hands to the side or behind her. Her serves either went into the net or soared out of bounds. She hit one spike that Noreen set up for her but missed two other easy chances.

At the end of the period Gail put the feedsack dress back on with reluctance. She looked around the locker room. Everyone else was wearing store-bought clothes, though some of them were a little faded. Only half a dozen girls were dressed as nicely as Veronica and her shadow, Linda. Four of them were clustered together on the other side of a wall of baskets.

Most of the girls left, but Gail fought to comb the tangles out of her hair,

"I won't play if she's captain," Linda said, her voice soft but carrying easily to Gail. "I could fill a whole slam book on her. She's nothing but a slut, the way she runs around with all those high school boys."

"Kenny is the only one she's dating," another girl

said. "His mother told my mother he's crazy about her."

"Then he's crazy period," Linda answered. "He better be careful. She'll get pregnant just like her big sister did and there'll be another shotgun wedding. You know, Noreen left town last summer at the same time Kenny went to visit his brother. I'll bet they really went together to some cabin down in the Ozarks."

Hot with anger that Linda would start such an awful rumor, Gail turned to rush down the aisle where Veronica's gang was huddled.

"Maybe she's already pregnant," Veronica said.

Mrs. Ransler's warning about self-control and letting teachers handle the discipline flashed through Gail's mind, but she couldn't let Linda think she was getting away with her lies.

Smirking, Linda was leaning back against a locker with her feet in the aisle.

Gail saw opportunity. "Excuse me," she said sweetly. She planted the heel of her left foot firmly on the shiny toe of one of Linda's black-and-white saddle oxfords.

Linda yelped in pain.

"Oh, did I hurt you?" Gail shifted her weight to her right heel and stepped on the other white toe. "I'm so sorry." She headed for the door leading to the hall where the rest of the class stood chatting and waiting for the bell.

Relieved that no one had heard Linda's words or cry of pain, Gail decided she couldn't tell Noreen, or anyone

Chapter Nine

else, what she'd heard. Just repeating it might make someone think it was true.

Walking to general science, Gail wondered what Noreen would have done if she'd overheard Linda. How do you fight vicious gossip? Stepping on Linda's toes had felt good but solved nothing. Being called shabby seemed small potatoes now.

By the time she took her seat between O.T. and Noreen in social studies, Gail had forgotten her own problems and was worrying about Noreen's.

O.T. leaned toward her and whispered, "What are you going to do tomorrow morning?"

"About what?"

"About apologizing, of course."

"Oh, that," Gail said indifferently. "Nothing."

Noreen looked up from her *True Confessions*. "You sure recover fast."

Mrs. Ransler frowned at them, and the three opened their notebooks.

"All right, class. Today we're going to talk about what the Bill of Rights means to us in 1949. Which right do you think is the most important, Noreen?"

Noreen closed her notebook, covering her magazine. "The first—freedom of speech, religion, assembly, and petition."

"Why?"

"Because it's first. A lot of people never read very far,

so the founding fathers put the most important one in the beginning."

Gail thought Linda had gone far beyond freedom of speech.

Mrs. Ransler looked at O.T. "Do you agree with Noreen?"

The class stirred. Mrs. Ransler almost never called on students without giving everyone a chance to volunteer first.

He looked at Gail. "I think the ones guaranteeing the rights of the accused are pretty important."

Mrs. Ransler swept her eyes around the room as several students snickered. "What do you say to that, Gail?"

On the spot, Gail thought for a moment. "I think Noreen and O.T. both make good points, but what I'd like to know is when do we teenagers get these rights?" Frustration pushed her on. "We're not tried by a jury of our peers. We don't have freedom to assemble at noon. What good does the Bill of Rights do us?" She stopped, afraid that, once again, she'd gone too far.

Mrs. Ransler nodded. "Interesting question, maybe one you could consider for the radio show. Does anyone have an answer?"

Veronica held up her hand. "Those who are mature and responsible hold our rights in trust. I certainly wouldn't want to be governed by the people in this room."

After what Gail had heard in the gym, she almost agreed with Veronica, but Gail was in no mood to admit

Chapter Nine

that. "Even if you had a vote, too?"

"Not even if I had two votes," Veronica answered.

"Yes, a good subject for the radio panel," Mrs. Ransler said. "By the way, Veronica, what do you have to report from your meeting this morning?"

Gail sighed. In the fuss over the egg, she and Noreen had missed the meeting.

Veronica cleared her throat. "The panel members present elected me chairman and voted unanimously to meet after school one evening a week to work on the show."

Chapter Ten

Gail's heart beat so hard she feared others could hear it. She looked at Noreen for guidance, but the dark-haired girl continued sketching a Scottish terrier in the margin of her notebook.

"Say something," O.T. hissed. "Don't let Veronica get away with it."

Mrs. Ransler strolled over to stand in front of the three but didn't look at them. "I'd like to have a little talk with you after school, Veronica."

Veronica nodded, her face clouded.

When the bell finally set them free, Gail dashed to her locker and out to the bus. She followed Alice to a back seat and pretended not to notice that Red was sitting across from them.

"I was just dying to talk to you all afternoon," Alice

Chapter Ten

said breathlessly. "Did you really knock down the principal's son?"

"No, but I did manhandle him a bit," Gail admitted, not at all proud of it. She told Alice the story, with her audience growing to include all seven junior high students.

"What are your folks goin' to say?" Alice asked, her eyes wide.

Gail had tried not to think about that. "Maybe I won't have to tell them."

"Your mother is bound to ask about the spot on your dress," Pete pointed out. "Will you make up something?"

"No. I won't lie to them." With less assurance, she added, "They'll understand."

Everyone looked skeptical.

Alice broke an awkward silence: "At least we can look forward to getting our checks from the fair today."

Gail sighed. "My check won't even buy paper and pencils."

Pete laughed. "Red's the money man. When are you goin' to spend all that money, millionaire?"

Red's face was grim. "Tomorrow."

Although she wondered what he could possibly be doing with so much money that could make him so sad, Gail pretended she didn't care. She turned to face Alice, ignoring the murmur of the two boys' voices.

At supper Gail told her family about sitting on the

egg. She made light of it, saying it was just silly kids' stuff. It was harder to laugh off the principal sentencing her to detention until she apologized to her homeroom.

"He has to keep discipline," her mother said after exchanging glances with her husband. "You can apologize tomorrow morning and the whole thing will be over."

Gail took a deep breath. "I told the principal I would apologize to the class when whoever put the egg in my chair apologizes to me."

Her father reached for the pitcher of lemonade. "None of the kids will tell the principal who did it, of course. Nobody wants to be a tattletale. You must suspicion who it was, though."

"Yes, but I don't know for sure."

Bobby held out his glass for more lemonade. "Does everybody know you'll be detentioned until you say you're sorry?"

Gail nodded. "Word is spreading pretty fast."

"They'll admit it tomorrow then," her mother said.

Bobby shook his head. "I bet they don't. You'll have to apologize or be stuck in there all year."

"Then I'll be stuck," Gail said.

Her father raised an eyebrow at her mother.

She speared another slice of tomato. "Gail, I wish you'd think this through rather than just digging in your heels like that mule at the fair. After all, you did fly off the handle and get the wrong person to boot."

Chapter Ten

They left the matter there, but as Gail finished her homework in the living room, she knew her parents were talking about her in the porch swing.

The next morning Gail walked into homeroom determined to stick to her resolution—and to look in her chair before she sat down.

The class quieted the instant the bell rang.

Mrs. Ransler checked the roll and looked around the room. "Does anyone have anything special to say today?"

No one responded.

"I'll be asking that question each morning until I get the answer I want. The sooner it comes, the better for everyone." She paused, but no one spoke. "Very well. We have to elect a captain for the girls' volleyball team. Only the players can vote." She read the names of twelve girls and called for nominations.

Margie waved her hand. "I nominate Noreen. She's our best player."

"Second," someone said.

Noreen closed the book she'd been reading. "I was captain last year. It's somebody else's turn."

"That's right," Veronica said. "I nominate Linda. She plays great."

"Second," the girl next to Linda said.

On a secret ballot, Noreen won six to five. One ballot was blank.

Pretty sure it was Noreen's, Gail wondered why the star athlete wouldn't want to be captain.

When the bell rang, Mrs. Ransler stopped Gail and Noreen. Speaking in a low voice, she said, "The radio panel chairman and I agreed that you'll be meeting during the noon hour rather than after school."

Gail nodded. It didn't really matter. She couldn't meet then either.

In English class that morning, Red didn't answer when the teacher called the roll.

"He's at the hospital," Pete said. "His mother is having an operation today."

Forgetting she was in class, Gail turned around in her chair, "Is it serious?"

"Real serious."

Gail's heart sank. What a jerk she'd been! Acting like a spoiled child because some people had laughed at her. She remembered that Red had talked about the need for health insurance the first day of school. His family had needed that money from the fair for his mother's operation. Gail scolded herself for the times at the fair when she was angry with Red and for the times since then that she'd thought only about herself. She should have realized something big was bothering Red.

"Gail!" Miss Clegmyer stood right in front of her. "Please join us."

Chapter Ten

The class tittered.

"I'm sorry. I wasn't listening."

The teacher's mouth formed an O of surprise, and she frowned. Then her face softened. "Perhaps you can call the hospital from the office at noon to see how your friend's mother is doing. Now, however, please pay attention."

Gail nodded, but she had no intention of intruding on the Royces, not even with words of sympathy.

At noon, she took her algebra book into her private cell, but she couldn't concentrate on the numbers. Instead she thought of Red, who might lose his mother, and of Noreen, who had already lost her mother. Tears welled up in her eyes as she thought how awful life would be for her and Bobby if anything happened to their mother.

Yet Red hadn't dropped a hint of his worry, except through his focus on winning the money. Because she had been too set on herself to ask. Her admiration for his courage and her shame at her own selfishness grew side by side.

When Mrs. Ransler put a hand on Gail's shoulder, she almost jumped out of her chair.

"Gail, I can see you don't like to back down when you think you're right, but you should think whether your refusal to apologize is worth the price. After all, it's not hurting anyone but you."

With a wave of her hand, Gail dismissed the warning. "That's not important compared to—other people's problems." Neither Red nor Noreen would appreciate her discussing their difficulties with the teacher.

Mrs. Ransler sat down in the chair next to Gail. "You mean Noreen. It's hard to understand why a girl as intelligent and talented as Noreen arouses so much antipathy, isn't it?"

"Antipathy?"

"Antagonism, dislike. Several girls told me they won't play on the homeroom team if she's captain. They want me to ask her to resign 'for the sake of the homeroom.'"

Gail clenched her fist, and she wanted to use it. "Why are they so mean?"

The teacher looked away for a long moment. "Do you think she anticipated this and tried to avoid it this morning?"

Gail could hardly believe Mrs. Ransler was talking to her like an equal, like someone who could and would help another student. "Yes, I'm sure she did, and probably all the girls who voted for her knew, too. I don't understand why some girls say bad things about her and treat her like this."

The teacher smiled. "I have a lot more life experience than you do, and I still don't understand it. I have learned that being different is always difficult, especially if you attract attention and envy, if you threaten others' status or territory."

Gail swallowed. She sensed the teacher was talking about her as well as Noreen. But Gail couldn't see why anyone would envy her or how she threatened anyone. Feeling lost, she asked, "But how do you deal with these mean people if you're different? Do you fight back? Or crawl in a hole? Or pretend it doesn't matter?"

Chapter Ten

Mrs. Ransler sighed. "All of the above, I suppose. You're not just learning English and history and math at school. You're learning to deal with other people." She patted Gail's hand. "And we all spend a lifetime learning to deal with ourselves."

Gail studied the teacher's sympathetic face, thinking, "She's one of those different people, too."

The bell ended their talk, but Gail continued to think about it as she went to study hall. She had tried to deal with the egg in her chair with force—an eye for an eye—and Noreen pretended to ignore trouble, to not care. Neither response seemed to work well.

Gail loved being in the barn-sized, high-ceilinged study hall and library. Students sat at rows of tables with chairs for six, but only two to four students at each. Windows with bookshelves under them lined one wall. At one end the librarian sat at a huge desk by the card catalogue. Beyond her were rows of six-foot-high bookshelves. At Gail's grade school, one big metal cabinet had held the entire library.

Noreen took her usual seat by Gail and opened the book she'd been reading in homeroom that morning.

Pretending to review her general science lesson, Gail thought, "I can't ask her about this captain business, but maybe I can give her a chance to talk about her problems. That's what I should've done with Red."

Making sure the white-haired but keen-eared librarian was occupied at her desk, Gail whispered, "What are you reading?"

Noreen's eyes stayed on the page. "*Grapes of Wrath.*" She sounded defiant.

"What's it about?"

"A bunch of Oklahoma farmers leaving the Dust Bowl to go to California."

That sounded pretty dull to Gail. "There are so many books here, and you read a lot. Could you suggest one?"

Noreen looked up. "Miss Watson has a list of recommended books at her desk."

"Is that book on the list?"

Noreen shrugged. "I never look at the list." She lowered her eyes to the page.

Gail went to the desk and asked for the list. She'd never heard of most of the books on it and found reading titles a poor way to choose a book. She smiled to see that Noreen's book not only was on the list but also was marked for advanced readers.

Gail treated herself to browsing the shelves. She finally chose *Lion in the Streets,* a novel about politics. She had just become engrossed in the story when Noreen nudged her and turned the book so she could see the title.

She nodded approvingly. "Is that on the list?"

"I don't know, but your book is. Let me know when you turn it in."

Noreen hesitated. "Steinbeck writes strong stuff, but then that book isn't exactly *The Bobbsey Twins at the Seashore*

Chapter Ten

either. Did you know it's really about Huey Long, that crooked governor who was assassinated in the Thirties? Sometimes people are really stupid about who they elect. If you don't believe me, just wait until our class elections."

Gail read on, eager to find out what Noreen meant by "strong stuff." Gail wished she dared read in classes the way Noreen did.

When Gail went outside to meet the bus, Red was there, even though he hadn't been in social studies. The freckles on his cheeks stood out against his pale skin.

She rushed up to him. "How's your mother?"

"The doctor says she'll be okay, but she has to take it easy for a coupla months. Dad's staying with her tonight. I'm going home to do the chores."

A weight slid off Gail's shoulders. "I'm so glad she's okay. And Red, I'm awfully sorry I was so silly about your not helping me with Caribou. I understand now why Huckleberry being the Grand Champion was so important."

She'd hoped for a big smile and a renewal of the friendship they had begun at the fair. Instead Red's face remained grim. When they got on the bus, he took a seat as far away from her as he could get.

Chapter Eleven

Late Sunday afternoon Gail's mother brought the feedsack dress into her daughter's bedroom and hung it on the hook on the door.

"I know it's Sunday, but I got your morning glory dress washed and ironed so you could have your prettiest outfit to wear for your demonstration tomorrow." Her face glowed with satisfaction.

Sprawled on the bed reading her novel, Gail lowered her eyes to the page. "I don't think I'll wear that, Mom. The kids would giggle about my sitting on the egg."

"But wearing the dress will be good, since you're demonstrating how to take out stains. Besides, nothing else that's clean is half as pretty as this."

Gail forced a smile. "Thanks, Mom."

She kept reading to stop herself from speculating

Chapter Eleven

what disaster the dress would bring the next day.

When she stepped onto the bus the next morning, she was thinking about Red rather than the dress. He turned to look out the window as she got to where he and Pete were sitting. Disappointed, she went on by without saying anything.

Alice greeted Gail with a big smile, and Gail responded by complimenting her on her new dress.

Alice smoothed down the skirt of her pink and white striped seersucker dress. "Those town kids got so many nice clothes. I told Mother she just had to make something else for me."

Gail barely listened to the long story about selecting the cloth and thread and pattern. Instead she studied Alice's familiar round, red-cheeked face and the soft, light brown hair curling naturally around it. Yes, Alice was pretty, and she had enough clothes to wear something different to school every day for almost two weeks. She was smart, too, but she learned only what the teacher assigned. Shy in the new surroundings, she stuck mostly with the other country kids, but she acted happy.

Gail finally got a chance to talk. "We're starting our third week already. How do you like junior high?"

"It's okay, except for all the homework. I'm glad I don't have Mrs. Ransler. They say the principal gives her the best students and she makes 'em work like dogs."

That wasn't what Gail wanted to know. "How do you like the kids in your classes? Are they pretty nice?"

The Feedsack Dress

"They don't go out of their way to make you feel welcome, but they don't bother me. None of Veronica's crowd even knows my name, I'm sure." She laughed. "Nobody has put an egg in my chair yet."

Gail smiled, but her frustration grew as she saw that her experience had been so different from Alice's and couldn't see why. She pondered that question while nodding in response to Alice's chatter the rest of the way to school.

For the first time since school started, Noreen was already in her chair fanning herself with a piece of paper when Gail arrived in homeroom.

"I got our volleyball tournament schedule."

"I won't be able to play." Gail grinned. "That should help the team."

Noreen smiled back. "You're not exactly rookie of the year, but we just might need you." Her face sobered.

As soon as Mrs. Ransler took the roll, Noreen asked permission to read the schedule. "I'd like to see the hands of those who can play our first game, on Friday." All the players except Gail, Veronica, and Linda held up their hands.

O.T. twisted around to look at Linda. "What's with you? You were one of our best players last year."

"Mind your own business for a change," she snapped.

Mrs. Ransler gave both warning looks.

O.T. turned his attention to the paper bag Gail had brought to homeroom. "Whatcha got?"

"The junk for my demonstration in speech. I'm going

Chapter Eleven

to show how to remove stains from clothes."

He grinned. "Good thing for you and me to know."

Gail grinned back. O.T. was silly sometimes, but he wasn't mean. She wished she could have made up with Red this easily.

In spite of Gail's worry about a new disaster, the demonstration went well. She put three stains—catsup, ink, and motor oil—on a strip from a worn-out dress and showed how to use cool water, chlorine bleach, and corn meal to remove them. She'd rehearsed it a dozen times, and working with her hands relieved her of the anxiety of facing her audience.

"Well done, Gail," Miss Harlan said. "You've obviously done demonstrations in 4-H. Just one thing: You need to have better eye contact with your audience. Pick out friendly faces in various parts of the room and look at those people as you speak."

Gail nodded and began to put her materials back in her sack.

"Does anyone have any questions?"

Veronica whispered something to Phil, and he raised his hand.

"How do you take out egg?"

"The same way I take bad words off the tongues of gossips, with soap and water," Gail flashed back.

The laugh came at Phil's expense.

Two girls asked serious questions, and Gail managed

to answer them.

Veronica raised her hand. "Do these methods work on anything but feedsacks?"

Gail's heart accelerated, but she swallowed her anger and said calmly, "These methods will work with all fairly sturdy cottons."

Gail managed to avoid Veronica until sixth period when Mrs. Ransler released the students on the radio panel to meet in her office-storage room the last few minutes of social studies.

Because the little room held only two chairs, Gail followed Noreen's example of perching on the book-laden table. Veronica and a short, curly-haired boy named Arthur took the chairs. Ralph, a tall, needle-thin boy in glasses, leaned against the wall.

For a minute no one spoke. Then Ralph opened a notebook. "I guess we oughta talk about what we're going to do."

Veronica looked out the window rather than at her fellow students. "Any suggestions?"

Noreen pulled out a nail file and began to smooth a nail on her left hand.

Gail guessed that the others had no more idea about what was expected of them than she did. That didn't make her feel any better.

Ralph took a stubby pencil from behind his ear. "We had an interesting discussion in class about how important

Chapter Eleven

the Bill of Rights is to us today."

Veronica shook her head. "That's too boring."

Ralph straightened. "Our topic is citizenship. We're not producing *The Green Hornet*."

"Fine. We'll vote on it," Veronica said. "All in favor put up your hands."

Ralph and Gail raised their hands.

"All opposed."

Veronica and Arthur raised their hands.

Gail groaned inside her head.

"Tied," Veronica said. "Noreen, you have to vote with us since you didn't vote when I called for those in favor."

Noreen shook her head without looking up from her filing. "I'm abstaining. I don't care what we do as long as we don't waste time on it."

"Stalemate," Arthur announced. "Let's kick around some other possibilities."

Veronica bestowed a smile on him. "Good idea. What would you like to do?"

They discussed and discarded half a dozen vague ideas.

Mrs. Ransler opened the door. "What topic are you proposing?"

"None," Ralph answered. "We voted on only one, and we split down the middle on that."

The teacher sighed. "I chose five students so you couldn't split down the middle. This radio show is a great opportunity for you and the school. I'm relying on you."

The Feedsack Dress

Noreen put away her nail file. "The Constitution guarantees the right to vote. It doesn't say you have to use it."

"Then I will usurp the right you chose to forfeit, which is just what happens in the real world. What was the topic proposed?"

She voted for it as the bell rang.

"I have to catch the bus," Gail reminded them, heading for the door.

Mrs. Ransler stopped her. "You can all go, but I want you to meet here again tomorrow morning during homeroom to decide exactly what you'll focus on."

Tuesday, Wednesday, and Thursday mornings, the group met for five minutes of their ten-minute homeroom period. Each time Veronica pooh-poohed every idea Ralph and Gail suggested, Arthur agreed, and Noreen refused to vote.

"Darn it, Noreen," Gail said in exasperation as the bell ending homeroom rang Thursday morning. "You'll have to take sides sometime."

When they reported no progress, Mrs. Ransler threw up her hands. "This is the slowest committee I ever saw, and believe me, that's saying something. To simplify matters, each of you research two amendments this weekend, come together next week, and plan the show. I'll let you girls miss social studies and get the boys out of study hall that hour. If you don't pull everything together then, I'm canceling the whole

Chapter Eleven

thing."

Friday morning, Gail went to homeroom relieved she wouldn't have to face the struggle with Veronica and Arthur, but Gail's good mood disappeared when Mrs. Ransler came to Noreen just before the bell and told her that two girls said they couldn't play volleyball that day.

Her face neutral, Noreen didn't even ask who they were. Watching her, Gail thought the defections didn't matter—until she heard a snap and saw Noreen had broken her pencil in two.

When the teacher finished calling the roll, Noreen raised her hand. "We don't have enough players today, so we have to forfeit our first game." She took a deep breath, but her voice remained calm. "As captain, recruiting players is my responsibility. I'm resigning so those who signed up to play can elect a new captain."

Margie shot out of her seat. "We don't need a new captain. We need some team spirit. Twelve people signed up. Monday we had nine players, one extra. Today we're one short. I know why Gail can't play, but I'd like to hear why the other four can't."

"Me, too," O.T. chimed in. "The team is supposed to represent all of us." He glared at Veronica. "We'll remember how you let us down when we elect class officers."

Veronica glared back. "We've been invited to a fashion show at a country club luncheon. We can't play."

O.T. turned to Gail. "Are you going to let them pull

this? The team needs one more player."

Gail felt trapped. "But I'm no good even if I did play."

"All we need is a body," Margie pleaded. "Besides—well, you know what I mean."

Gail knew exactly what she meant. Veronica and Linda were leading a mutiny to humiliate Noreen. But apologizing would be giving in to them, too. She looked to Mrs. Ransler for help, but the teacher was studying her roll book.

"I know what's stopping you, Gail," O.T. whispered. "You're half Missouri mule and half martyr about that detention." He stood up. "Mrs. Ransler, I'm apologizing to Gail and to the class for putting that egg in her chair."

Amazed, Gail muttered, "Don't be silly. Everyone knows you didn't do it."

"You got your public apology," O.T. said, and he looked as stern as his father. "Now it's your turn."

Chapter Twelve

Gail thought of the eight lunches she had eaten alone in the homeroom to prove a point. Then she thought of the broken pencil Noreen had just hidden in her magazine. O.T. had seen how hurt Noreen was, and he'd been willing to pay a price to help her. Gail could do no less.

She rose and faced the class. "I apologize to all of you, and especially to O.T."

Mrs. Ransler beamed. "Thank you both. I'll let Mr. Addison know. You have a full team, Noreen."

Gail sat down. "You wouldn't say that if you'd ever seen me play."

Noreen smiled at her. "You'll do okay."

"Now we got a *real* team," Margie crowed.

Linda rolled her eyes. "Yeah, real losers."

"Girls! That's enough!" Mrs. Ransler cautioned, and

her tone closed their lips. "Remember, Raiders, you should eat a light lunch before a game."

By the time the bell for lunch rang, Gail didn't feel like eating at all. All morning Veronica's gang made nasty cracks about what a bad team their homeroom had without them. What galled Gail was that they were right, and she could do nothing about it.

Gail's teammates had heard the comments, too, and worked up a head of steam. When Gail went to the locker room, Margie, five feet tall and ninety pounds, was urging her teammates to show the snobs what the peasants could do.

Noreen, already in her gym clothes, ignored everyone and focused on a clipboard. She handed it to a high school girl wearing a black-and-white striped referee vest and called the Raiders to huddle around her in one corner of the locker room.

"They've got a stronger team, so we have to be smarter than they are," she said softly. She ticked off the strengths and weaknesses of the girls on the other team and laid out a strategy for dealing with their serves. Then she showed her own players where she had placed them in the three-two-three formation. She placed Gail in the middle of the back three, making her the last team member to serve.

"I'll be playing right next to you," Noreen told Gail. "I'll take your balls. You just keep out of my way."

Margie nodded. "We'll all cover for you, Gail. Don't worry about it."

Chapter Twelve

Noreen patted Gail on the shoulder. "You just give us a coupla good spikes from the front row, kid."

Gail flinched a little at the "kid." She knew she seemed young and naive to Noreen, who couldn't be more than fourteen to her thirteen.

Until the last minute of the first half, Gail didn't touch a ball. Noreen played not only her own and Gail's balls but also half of all the others. Noreen and tiny but fierce Margie ruled the floor.

Inevitably it came time for Gail to serve. She fidgeted at the line, turning the ball around in her left hand as she worked up her courage to hit it.

"Just try to get it over the net," Noreen said.

Gail swung her right arm, and her fist connected squarely with the ball. It floated over the net, and a Horror on the front row spiked it. The half ended with the Horrors leading the Raiders fifteen to eleven.

"We're doin' great," Margie shouted as the teams changed sides of the net for the second half. "Let's get those four points right now."

"Right," another girl said, "'cause if we don't get them on Noreen's serve, we never will."

Their captain served five hard drives that fell untouched by the opposing players.

Feeling safe in the back row next to Noreen, Gail relaxed, but on the sixth serve, the ball came back hard straight at her knees. As a reflex Gail hit it with the palm of her right hand, and Margie fell to her knees on the front row to get it up in the air so Noreen could smash it.

Gail's goof drew the Horrors' attention, and they directed most of their returns to her. Two serves later, a ball she couldn't avoid bounced off her hands and out of bounds.

Gail's discomfort turned to humiliation. "Geez. I'm sorry, Noreen."

"Never mind, kid. Just get out of the way next time."

With a three-point lead to protect, the Raiders played hard. Although none could score, they kept the Horrors from winning points. Rotated to the front row, Gail surprised everyone, especially herself, with a successful spike. That brought Noreen up to serve again, but the opposition's well-placed spike ended her turn without a score.

When the official warned that only a minute remained, the Raiders still led by one point, but the Horrors' best player was serving. She served two quick points before Noreen, darting from the back row to the net, spiked Margie's set-up.

Margie grabbed the ball and shot it to Gail.

Noreen shoved Gail behind the serving line and yelled, "Quick! Just get it over."

Gail swung at the ball hard and felt intense relief as it sailed high over the net. She sank to her knees as it sailed out of bounds.

"Game!" called the official. "Harlan's Horrors over Ransler's Raiders twenty-four to twenty-three."

Gail trotted off the court blinking back tears of

Chapter Twelve

frustration. She almost collided with Mr. Addison as she headed across the hall to the locker room. Once there she splashed cold water from the big circular sink over her hot face and wished she could follow it right down the drain.

"I'm awful sorry I lost the game for us," she squeaked out as her teammates joined her.

Margie slapped her on the back. "Don't be silly. The team lost the game, not you."

"We put up a damn good fight," Noreen said, throwing water on her tomato-red face and her sweat-soaked blouse. "I never figured we could come this close without Linda and Veronica. But hell, I don't care if they never come back. This was fun!"

Gail couldn't believe her ears. "Fun? More like agony. I flinched every time a ball came at me."

The Horrors also had gathered around the sink. One turned to Gail, "Were you really that afraid the ball would hit you?"

"No, I was afraid I would hit it."

Girls from both teams laughed, and for the first time since school started, Gail felt part of a group.

Noreen grinned at her. "You just need some practice. Let's get back in the gym so you can serve a few before P.E. starts."

The P.E. teacher stuck her head into the locker room and called, "Gail Albright. Come out here, please."

Puzzled, Gail stepped into the hall.

The Feedsack Dress

Mr. Addison was waiting. "I would like to speak to you for a moment."

Gail brushed her hair out of her eyes. She heard the door open and knew Margie and several other Raiders were standing right behind her. "In your office, you mean?"

"No, here." He straightened his tie with nervous fingers. "It's only fitting that I apologize to you in public, since that's what I told you to do. Mrs. Ransler informed me that my—that O.T.—confessed to the class that he put the egg in your chair. I apologize for the excessive duration of your detention. I assure you that O.T. will be punished both for his thoughtless prank and for his inexcusable lie."

Incredulous, Gail shook her head. "I appreciate your apology, sir, but the one who really deserves it now is O.T. He didn't lie to you. One of the girls put that egg in my chair."

Chapter Thirteen

Mr. Addison's eyes opened wide. He took a white handkerchief from his breast pocket and dabbed at his forehead. "I think you had better come to my office after all."

"Right now?" Gail looked down at her sweat-soaked gym clothes.

"Yes." Taking her elbow, he strode toward his office.

Gail kept up, thankful that the bell hadn't rung yet and only the volleyball players could see her.

"I'm not to be disturbed," the principal told his secretary as he guided Gail into his office. He motioned her to the chair in front of his desk and pulled up another one rather than barricading himself behind his desk. "So O.T. wasn't lying to me. Then how do you explain his confession?"

His face and voice were almost pleasant, but this unfamiliar look didn't assure Gail. She took time to choose her words: "I think you should ask O.T."

His lips curved into a tight smile. "Oh, I shall, but I want to hear your opinion, since you didn't hesitate to defend the little scamp."

"It's kinda complicated." Gail decided to say as little as possible about it. "Our volleyball team was short one player. O.T. didn't want the team to have to forfeit, so he apologized to me so I would have to apologize to the class."

"Thus ending your detention and giving your team the player it needed." He rose and went to the window. He looked out for a long time before he turned around. "I don't understand why you were the only one who could play. Your homeroom has at least fifteen girls in it."

Gail said nothing.

"Tell me, Abigail, how do you know O.T. didn't put the egg in your chair?"

"He told me."

He sat down again. "And, of course, you know who did it."

Alarm bells went off in Gail's head. No one likes a tattletale. She had enough enemies already. She told the exact truth: "Not really, but I'm sure it wasn't O.T."

He studied her face. "It would be helpful to me, and to the guilty person in the long run, if you would tell me who was responsible."

Gail thought of what Veronica and Linda were doing to Noreen and how they deserved to be punished. Tempted

Chapter Thirteen

to tell how Veronica had been missing an egg for her demonstration, Gail held back instead. "I accused O.T. wrongly. I won't say anything about anyone else. Besides, it doesn't matter to me anymore."

"I could put you in detention again for refusing to tell me."

Gail sighed. This was as bad as losing the game.

He echoed her sigh. "I'm not going to. You may go to class." He opened the door for her.

O.T., waiting in the outer office, sprang to his feet.

"You can go to class, too, Sir Galahad."

As the principal closed his door, O.T. turned his eyes to heaven.

"You know," Gail said as they passed the secretary, "your father isn't as awful as I thought."

"No," O.T. said, his face dead serious for once, "he just acts that way sometimes. It's part of his job."

The secretary burst out laughing. "You two scat or you'll be late to class and have to come back here for excuse slips."

Gail hurried to the gym. As she half ran in the door, Margie tossed her a volleyball. Gail wished she could hit the thing as easily as she caught it.

Margie smirked. "Doesn't the warden want to see somebody else now?"

Everyone quieted, and Gail realized they had expected her to accuse Veronica of putting the egg in her chair. Gail almost said no, but Veronica deserved to squirm. "He doesn't tell me his business."

Noreen pushed Gail to the serving line. "Learning to serve is your business right now, kid. Our next game is Tuesday."

The teacher blew the whistle and told the girls to form groups of four to practice skills. Noreen rounded up Gail, Margie, and another girl from their homeroom team. The three focused on helping Gail practice until the teacher sent two groups to each side of the net. Noreen directed the Raiders to pass every ball they could to Gail, and Gail's turn to serve came every time one of the Raiders was supposed to serve.

The fourth time Gail served, the teacher noticed. She called Noreen over to the sidelines, spoke to her in a low voice, listened to her reply, and moved to the other side of the gym where other students were practicing. She stayed there the rest of the period, while Noreen continued to wave Gail to the serving line.

By the end of the period, Gail was getting the hang of serving. She couldn't send bullets across the net the way Noreen did or place the ball the way Margie did, but the ball went to the second row the last five times she hit it.

"You'll be a good player by the time we switch to aerial darts, Gail," Noreen said as they went to the locker room.

Gail groaned. "Aerial darts? I've never even heard of that. By the time I learn it, I suppose we'll go on to something else."

"Yup," Margie said. "After that, it's deck tennis, where

Chapter Thirteen

you throw a big rubber ring over the net."

"Gee whiz!" Gail foresaw an unending series of new humiliations. "I'm going to be a month behind everybody all year."

Margie slapped her on the back. "Naw, with Noreen coaching you, you'll only be three weeks behind."

Gail joined the laughter, just one of the group.

The feeling of belonging kept her smiling the rest of the day.

Saturday morning Gail and her father chased her pullets into the brooder house and spent a noisy half-hour catching them and putting them into crates. Harry Holt had offered to buy them for his flock. As they closed the last crate, Gail told her father how she'd felt after the volleyball game.

He smiled. "You get a special feelin' from bein' a spoke in a big wheel."

Together they carried the last crate to the pickup and hoisted it into the bed.

Her father pulled a bandana out of his back pocket and wiped his face. "I've been thinkin'. You must have been feelin' pretty much an outsider or this game wouldn't have made you feel so good."

Gail nodded, knowing that if she started to talk, her hurt and resentment would all pour out. She turned to take her seat in the pickup. She would have liked to clean up before delivering the chickens, but she'd just get dirty again unloading at the Holt's farm.

Her father climbed into the cab and started the motor. "Some of the town kids probably think farmers are bound to be dumb, but dumb kids didn't get picked to be on that radio show."

Gail smiled with satisfaction at the thought of that triumph.

"Got any particular friends among the town kids?"

Since her mother had suggested staying away from Noreen, Gail figured it wasn't smart to mention her now. "I'm pretty friendly with several kids, including O.T., the principal's son. He's not stuck up the way some of them are."

"You a little sweet on him?"

"Gosh no! He barely comes up to my chin."

He grinned. "How's Red?"

"He's been pretty worried about his mother." Gail's spirits plummeted. Red still avoided her on the bus and at school.

"Maybe you'll run into him on the square today. I don't reckon it'll take you long to find a new winter coat."

Gail knew he was right. The department store was the only place she could afford to shop, and she wouldn't find many coats at her price there. As they drove toward the Holt farm, she drew her father's attention to the neighbor's corn and grunted responses to his talk of bushels per acre and the price per bushel.

Although a hired hand took care of Harry Holt's

Chapter Thirteen

farmwork, the feedstore owner had come to supervise the chickens' move into their new home. He motioned for Gail's father to drive the pickup up next to a wire-fenced chicken yard.

Gail wondered if he would be as friendly as usual. After all, he'd side with his own granddaughter if she said mean things about the girl in the feedsack dress.

"Hi, there," he called as she climbed out of the cab. "How's my favorite farmer? Glad to get back to chickens after that tussle with the Royces' calf?"

She grinned sheepishly. "The chickens don't lead any better than Caribou did."

He peered into the crates. "I saw the ones you took to the fair, and these look just as good. Worth top dollar. I suppose you're goin' to buy a fancy new dress and suede shoes with your profits."

Gail barely managed to hold back, "I'm not Veronica." Forcing a smile to her lips, Gail said, "Naw, I need a coat and all the other winter stuff I've outgrown."

"The missus said the department store just got in some nice wool cloth. She got a pretty piece to make Veronica an outfit, but the girl threw a fit. She won't wear anything that doesn't come ready-made from some fancy store." He paused. "I expect you know my granddaughter. She tells me she's goin' to be elected class president this year."

So Veronica hadn't even mentioned Gail. "I know her, but I don't know anything about an election." Except that she'd never elect Veronica anything but skunk herder.

"They're goin' to be on a radio show together," her father said, pulling out a crate.

"Well, I'll be." Mr. Holt waved Gail away and took her end of the crate. "Veronica didn't tell me that, and here Holt Feeds is the sponsor. I'm sure glad to hear one of my customers will be on the show. Maybe I'll have you read one of my commercials, Gail."

"Sure. I'd be glad to." Gail almost laughed out loud. Veronica would be furious.

The unloading went quickly. When they finished, Mr. Holt handed Gail four tens and a five, a good five dollars more than she'd expected. She'd never had that much money, but she tried to act casual as she put it in the only hole-free pocket in her old jeans.

All the way home she tried to calculate how she'd spend it. As soon as they arrived, she grabbed the newspaper, a piece of scrap paper, and a pencil and ran to the kitchen where her mother was peeling apples for pie. Referring to the ads, they estimated, for the tenth time, the cost of what Gail would need.

"I think you better buy the smaller stuff first," her mother said. "You can spend whatever's left on the coat."

Gail added the odds and ends quickly. "Around twenty dollars left. Is that enough?"

Her mother sighed. "It will have to be."

Their afternoon of shopping started off well. At the

Chapter Thirteen

department store Gail got a pair of brown-and-white saddle oxfords for six dollars, rubber overshoes for two dollars, lengths of blue and gray wool material for two skirts for six dollars, a light blue sweater set for seven dollars, a bright red long-sleeved sweater for four dollars, and a pair of heavy wool gloves for a dollar. She wouldn't have many changes of clothes, but what she had would be nice.

"Gosh, Mom," Gail whispered as the cashier rang them up, "even with my fair money I've only got twenty-one dollars left, and I still need underclothes and jeans. That's another four dollars."

Alice waved at them through the front window and came into the store with a big smile. "Hi, Mrs. Albright. What did you buy, Gail?"

Gail displayed her new clothes with pleasure. Alice showed off two new sweaters from Stella's Style Shop. She suggested they go there to look for a coat.

Gail's mother shook her head. "I'm afraid Stella's is a little expensive."

"But they have some coats on sale," Alice said. "They're warmer than the ones here."

Gail shivered at the thought of waiting for the bus in the cold. "Come on, Mom. We could at least look."

Her mother frowned. "Be sensible, Gail. We'll look upstairs here first."

Mrs. Albright automatically led them to the rack with the cheapest coats, but most were too light for the cold winters. Gail admired a warm sky-blue coat with deep pockets, but it cost twenty-nine dollars.

"This navy blue one for twenty-four dollars isn't bad," her mother said, making Gail try it on for a second time. "I could take the sleeves up and move over the buttons this winter and let them out next year." She met Gail's eyes. "We have enough if I add my egg money to what you have."

Alice studied the coat with the critical eye developed in four years of 4-H sewing projects. "I think Stella has some coats for this price, Mrs. Albright. You could look at those and come back here if you don't find anything."

"Please, Mom. I'll be wearing the coat every single day."

Her mother smiled. "I guess it won't hurt to look."

Gail and Alice led the way out of the store and down the street toward Stella's with Alice chattering about the clothes she wanted to buy.

"That young woman is waving at you," Gail's mother said as they stood waiting for the traffic light to turn green.

The girls turned to look at a shiny red convertible, and Gail returned the wave as the car drove past them.

"It's Noreen," Alice said as they crossed the street. "I wish I had a boyfriend old enough to drive."

"And that he had a convertible," Gail added.

Her mother frowned. "That's the Boyle girl? She looks sixteen or seventeen. She's much too young to be drivin' around with a high school boy. I don't know what her father is thinking!"

Chapter Thirteen

Alice sobered. "Have you heard what some of the girls say about Noreen? About what she did last summer? And I saw in a slam book that she read a dirty book, *Raisins of Wrath,* right in class."

Gail wanted to kick her friend. "Alice! *Grapes of Wrath* is on the library's recommended list. Noreen's a nice person, and you shouldn't read slam books or listen to nasty gossip from a bunch of catty snobs."

"I—I didn't know she's a friend of yours," Alice stammered, blood darkening her rosy cheeks. "I'm just telling you what I heard."

"I've heard it, and I don't believe it. The girls spreading it just made it up."

Looking uncomfortable, Alice shrugged and hurried to Stella's window. "Isn't that plaid dress with all those shades of blue and violet just gorgeous? It would be perfect for you, Gail." She giggled. "I'll bet Red would sit next to you on the bus if you wore that."

Embarrassed, Gail glanced at her mother.

Smiling, she stopped to admire the dress. It had a white Peter Pan collar, a fitted bodice, and a full skirt.

"The plaids match exactly," her mother said. "That's so hard to do. And it matches your eyes."

Gail leaned against the window to read the price tag. $24.99. More than half of what she'd earned from working all summer. "But it doesn't match my budget." She knew going in would only emphasize what she couldn't afford, but she didn't want to admit that to Alice.

Gail led the way inside and went past the dresses to the back, where racks held three times as many coats as they'd seen at the department store. The three wandered between the rows looking for Gail's size.

A voice coming from the fitting room startled them. "How does this look in the back?"

Gail recognized Linda's voice.

"It fits you like a feedsack," came another voice, Veronica's. "Don't buy it unless you want to look like Shabby Abby."

"Ugh! Perish the thought!"

Heartsick and angry, Gail tried in vain to guide her mother away.

"I'd quit school if I had to wear the awful stuff she does," Linda said. "Are the Albrights dirt poor or are they just too dumb to know better?"

"Both. Guess what? She sold her chickens to Grandpa this morning. She told him she's going to use the money to buy her winter clothes. He thinks that's so great and I'm so extravagant. It makes me want to throw up. Can you imagine what she's going to buy with that chicken feed?"

Her mother's face turned white, the way it had when her favorite cow died. Gail gritted her teeth to keep from screaming at them to shut up.

"Let's go," her mother said softly, grabbing Gail's hand. "We'll look for a coat next week."

Chapter Thirteen

As they turned to leave, Gail saw Veronica look out from behind the curtain that served as a door to the fitting room.

"I really hate to shop on Saturdays," Veronica said. "That's when all the riffraff come to town."

Chapter Fourteen

Rage churned in Gail's stomach and turned her knees weak. She had never hated anyone or anything so much in her life. The depth of her hatred scared her, and she let her mother lead her from the store. Outside the store her mother dropped her hand and walked quickly to the corner, pausing only because cars blocked their path. Gail fought for self-control as she realized she was reacting exactly the way Veronica had wanted.

Gail's anger began to drain away when it occurred to her that Veronica was paying her back for stepping on Linda's toes. But that didn't justify her saying things to make the whole Albright family feel bad. Gail glanced at her mother, suddenly aware that her freshly ironed dress was made from the daisy feedsacks.

Her mother stared straight ahead, her face grim.

Chapter Fourteen

A few seconds later, Alice caught up with them. She'd been too far away to overhear Veronica and Linda's conversation. "Is something wrong? Are you goin' back to the department store already?"

"Not today," Gail's mother answered, and she gave her daughter a warning look. She pointed at the clock on the courthouse tower. "We're late. I have to get a new thimble at the dimestore before we meet Si and Bobby at Montgomery Ward's."

Alice walked with them across the square to the Woolworth's and on to Montgomery Ward's. All the time she talked about the new clothes she'd bought and the ones her mother was making and what she would wear when the weather turned cold. Gail wanted to yell at her to just shut up, but she knew that wasn't fair to Alice. Besides, Gail's mother's face wore the faint smile that signaled she was thinking rather than listening.

She kept that smile on her face as they shopped for groceries and drove home. Once there, she went into the bedroom and closed the door.

Gail made a point of showing her father and Bobby her pretty new clothes, but neither one bothered to pretend to be interested.

All evening Gail waited for her mother to say something about the cruel words they had overheard, but she said nothing.

After Gail went to bed that night, she heard the murmur of her parents' voices in the kitchen. Although she hated that Veronica had made her mother feel bad, Gail was relieved that she could stop pretending to like wearing the feedsack dress.

She sighed. She'd have to wear it anyway.

Sunday afternoon Gail took an old blanket and her social studies textbook out to the big elm tree in the front yard. A few minutes later her mother, carrying her mending basket and a pair of Bobby's jeans, came out of the house. "Will it bother you if I work here?"

"No. I was just thinking anyway."

"About what?" She sat down on the blanket.

"The Bill of Rights. I was assigned the ninth and the tenth for the radio panel."

Her mother blinked. "I can't remember what those two are."

"Neither can anybody else." Gail swallowed what she was thinking—that Veronica had given her the boring ones on purpose. "The ninth one says we aren't denied rights just because they aren't listed in the Constitution, and the tenth says the states and the people keep any rights the Constitution doesn't give to the national government or the states don't make illegal."

"Sounds kinda vague." Her mother threaded her needle. "I've been thinkin', too, sweetheart. Let's dye that dingy white blouse yellow."

Gail buried her face in the book to hide her lack of

Chapter Fourteen

enthusiasm. "Good idea."

"Your father and I decided to raise your allowance to fifty cents a week now that you're going to school in town."

"Thanks." Gail figured the extra dollar a month would help with pencils and paper but not with clothes.

Fitting a patch onto the knee of Bobby's jeans, her mother didn't look up. "Gail, you know we'd buy your clothes at Stella's if we could afford to, but for at least the next three years everything has to go into the farm."

Gail pictured the farm as a giant with a whip collecting tribute. Did her parents really have to give it every cent they made? She could accept that money was tight this year, but three years of being called Shabby Abby was too much. Even raising two hundred chickens next summer wouldn't give her enough money for store-bought clothes. She wished the sunny day would turn cloudy, the way she felt.

"Gail?"

She had to be an adult about it. "I know, Mom. Don't worry about what Veronica and Linda said. Those two get their kicks picking on people. Kids like that aren't worth worrying about."

Her mother put down her mending. "That's right, and I'm proud of you for being mature enough to realize that. Still—"

Mother and daughter sat silent—two women knowing that small humiliations can't be reasoned away.

Wanting to comfort her mother, Gail broke the silence: "Those skirts you're making will be real pretty with my new sweaters."

Her mother rose. "I'll go see if I've got that canary yellow dye for your blouse."

Gail watched her walk away in her faded feedsack blouse and a pair of raggedy cut-off jeans. Thinking about her mother's clothes for the first time, she realized that Flo Albright had been wearing the same two "good" dresses to funerals for years. She made all of her blouses and most of her dresses from feedsacks. The only new clothes she'd bought in the last year were a sweater, a pair of jeans, and a pair of shoes.

With difficulty, Gail forced herself to go back to the Bill of Rights.

The screen door slammed, and a moment later her father knelt by her blanket.

"Need some help with something, Dad?"

"Naw. I was just thinkin' that raise in your allowance ought to be what they call retroactive. We didn't realize how expensive junior high would be."

"I'll manage." That's what her mother always said when they talked money.

"Managin' isn't always good enough." He handed her a dollar bill and two quarters. "This will help a little on your winter coat. Maybe you'll want to get some other stuff, too. Flo says Alice is wearing lipstick now."

Gail really didn't care about lipstick. "I'd like to get a

Chapter Fourteen

pair of those heavy bobbysox. They'll be lots warmer than the regular anklets for winter."

"Yeah." He stood up. "I got to go grease the wagon, get it ready for corn pickin' next month."

As he walked off, Gail wondered what Veronica's parents were like to make their daughter grow up so mean. They sure couldn't be anything like her grandfather. Pulling her blanket deeper into the shade, she wished the weather would cool off so she could wear her new clothes.

"You'll be sick to death of them by spring, stupid," she scolded herself. She forced herself to think about the rights reserved to the people.

Boarding the bus Monday morning, Gail was hurt to see that Alice already had a seatmate, Pete.

Grinning, he pointed across the aisle to where Red was sitting. "Here's a seat."

It wasn't the only seat free, but Gail took it. She'd really missed sitting with him.

Red grunted a neutral greeting, his usual smile missing. His freckles stood out on his face, either because he was pale or because his summer tan was fading.

Unsure what to say, Gail took plenty of time arranging her books on her lap. "How's your mother? Has she come home from the hospital yet?"

"Not yet. Maybe on Wednesday." His face lost some of its grimness. "I'll have to do the cookin' and sweepin' up a while longer, but the doctor says she'll be fine."

Surprised that he would admit to doing women's work, Gail asked, "Are you a good cook?"

"Ma always had me fry the bacon, and I make a darn good chocolate cake," he said with pride. "She's goin' to teach me to do a bunch of other stuff when she gets home. I'm gettin' sick of bacon and eggs at every meal." At last he grinned. "I don't know whether to cackle or go out and root."

Gail laughed, and they talked about their disasters in the kitchen the rest of the way to school.

Even though the trip went fast, the bus was running late. Gail walked as fast as she dared to get to homeroom before the last bell. This time she looked before leaping into her chair.

O.T. was talking to someone in the next row and Noreen was reading a *True Confessions* magazine. Both noted Gail's caution and smiled. She smiled back, delighted that the feeling of belonging she'd had on Friday was still there.

Mrs. Ransler called for quiet. "We have several announcements today. Phil, come up front to give yours."

He took his time working his way down the second row and coming to the front. His posture spoke of confidence, but his smile was shy. "As last year's class president, I want to say that we'll have our first class meeting on Friday during sixth period. I appointed a nominating committee last spring, and they'll tell everybody about the candidates for the election."

O.T. waved his hand. "Did you nominate yourself for

president again?"

"I didn't qualify." He flexed his muscles. "The rules say this year the president has to be a girl. You put on a dress, and maybe somebody will nominate you, O.T."

Most of the students laughed, and Phil bestowed a smile on Veronica before walking back to his seat.

O.T. muttered, "Big goon thinks he's Superman because he's the only freshman on the high school football team."

Mrs. Ransler frowned at him and called on Noreen.

Gail glanced at O.T. Was he jealous of the tall, broad-shouldered athlete?

Noreen turned in her chair rather than standing. "We have a volleyball game tomorrow. I'd like to see the hands of those who can play."

Eight hands went up, and Noreen's grip on her pencil relaxed. "Good. We picked up a sub. Bring your lunches to the Jail tomorrow and we'll plan our strategy there."

"Are you predicting another big victory?" Linda sneered.

Making sure Mrs. Ransler wasn't looking, Margie flipped a tiny wad of paper at Linda with a rubber band. "We'll win by five points. If you and Veronica played, we'd lose by two."

Gail thought the extra player would get her off the hook, but when she went to P.E. that afternoon, Noreen was waiting for her at the locker room door.

"Hurry up! We need to work on set-up patterns before class starts."

"What are those?"

"You know, passing the ball to a teammate so they can kill it. Lots of times that's smarter than returning it yourself, especially if you're playing the back row."

"Team work," Margie said, glaring at Linda. "Something some people just can't seem to understand."

Noreen and Margie spent the entire class drilling Gail and the other Raiders on set-ups. Mrs. Chapelli walked by occasionally and pointed something out, but mostly she let the group alone.

For her part, Gail found playing volleyball about as much fun as working algebra problems. She always ran one step behind in both.

After dressing for her next class, she went up to Noreen and interrupted her reading of a movie magazine. "Why were you working me so hard? The team won't even need me tomorrow."

Noreen didn't even look up. "We had enough players last time, until the last minute. I'll put you in for a little while even if we still have nine tomorrow."

"Don't feel you need to do that," Gail hastened to assure her. "I don't mind."

The P.E. teacher stuck her head around the corner of one of the rows of lockers. "And miss her chance to show what a good teacher she is? I believe she's after my job."

Margie laughed so hard she had to sit down. "Imagine Noreen a teacher!"

Chapter Fourteen

"That doesn't take much imagination," Gail said quickly, as some of the other girls started to laugh.

Still giggling, Margie said, "How about it, Noreen? You gonna be a teacher?"

"And waste my time with spoiled brats who build themselves up by tearing everybody else down? No thanks."

Eyes widened as the words and the bitterness in Noreen's voice carried through the locker room

No one spoke.

"Fortunately, Noreen, those brats are always in the minority," Mrs. Chapelli said. "Every year a teacher finds at least one child who is special. That makes up for the dozens whose names you forget a month after school is out and the half dozen you remember because they're growing up to be bitches."

The girls gasped at the use of the forbidden word.

The teacher clapped her hand over her mouth. "I'm sorry, girls. I didn't mean to say that."

The bell rang and the girls filed into the hall.

Gail stopped to pick up half a pencil that fell out of Noreen's notebook. Handing it over, Gail said, "Well, I guess I know who a coupla the bitches are."

Noreen nodded. "And I know somebody who's special."

"Who?"

"Ask that red-headed cowboy."

Chapter Fifteen

Special to Red? Gail couldn't get the thought—the wish, she admitted—out of her head. Walking out of the school to catch the bus, she slowed so that Pete and Alice would get on ahead of her. As she'd hoped, they sat down together. Gail slid into the empty seat across from them and held her breath as Red came down the aisle.

He hesitated a moment as he drew near, and she smiled. He sat down by her.

Happiness warming her whole body, she sat tongue-tied.

Red turned to ask Pete about some wood for their industrial arts class. When he turned back, Gail groped desperately for something to say. "How do you like shop?"

He shrugged. "It's a waste of time really. I've been workin' with tools all my life." He grinned. "I'd rather take a

Chapter Fifteen

class that's got some girls in it."

She went numb. Was Red telling her he liked all girls? That she was nothing special? "How—how do you like school in general?"

"So-so." He considered a moment. He never seemed to rush into things the way she did. "I sure hated it at first, but now it's okay. The only class I really like is general science. Mr. Wilkins treats you like you got some sense even when you ask stupid questions. Plus, I'm doin' a project with Ralph. He's a real nice guy. His father's a doctor so Ralph knows a lot of science stuff."

"You mean the skinny Ralph on my radio panel?"

"Yep. I sure gave him h-e-double-toothpick for voting to have the panel meetings after school. He said he didn't know you ride the bus. He thought you were new in town."

Gail felt better about Ralph. "Veronica knew."

"Aw, don't let her get your goat. Ralph says she's always been a spoiled brat. He says she'll get even worse if she gets elected class president." He glanced down at the reading textbook in her lap. "Boy, I sure liked that 'Lady and the Tiger' story. Even Miss Clegmyer couldn't ruin that one."

Gail relaxed as they talked about homework. She didn't even notice they had reached her stop.

"Hey, Gail," the driver yelled. "Don't you want to get off the bus tonight?"

Gail wanted to say, "No, I don't. I want to stay right

here." Instead, cheeks burning, she hurried off the bus.

The next morning the seat next to Red was empty, and Gail's heart skipped with happiness as he made a show of picking up his books so she could sit by him.

"That's a real pretty yellow you dyed your blouse," Red said.

Gail was glad he'd noticed but sorry he'd recognized the blouse. At least she knew he paid attention to what she looked like. She hesitated a moment before confiding, "Mom overheard Veronica and Linda make some nasty remarks about—about country kids' clothes last Saturday. She thought the dye might make this blouse look less like a hand-me-down."

Red nodded, his face grim. "Some of the guys were calling me General Mills because of my flour-sack shirts. I told 'em if they were goin' to call me General, they'd better salute. That stopped it."

Gail reflected that the boys could be as mean as the girls. To change the subject, she said, "My homeroom team has a big volleyball game at noon."

"I'll come watch."

Gail flinched at the thought of his seeing her play. "Please don't. I'm the worst one on the team."

He shook his head. "I'm glad to know you're not tops at everything."

She assumed he wouldn't come, but when Ransler's Raiders trotted out to warm up, Red stood at the edge of the

Chapter Fifteen

court with Ralph, O.T., and a dozen or so other boys.

Pretending not to see them, Gail tried in vain to concentrate on the ball rather than her coming humiliation in front of Red. When a ball bounced off her hands and out of bounds, she gave up. "Noreen, I'd rather not play today. I'm not good enough yet, and you've got eight without me."

Noreen glanced at the boys. "We can't disappoint your rooting section. You'll play the first half."

As in the first game, Noreen played all over the court, but she let Gail play two easy balls and then, when they had rotated to the front row, set up a spike that Gail pounded between opponents.

Noreen grinned and whispered. "That should impress Red." She was much more relaxed than she had been during the first game, perhaps because the Raiders maintained a five-point lead gained from her first turn serving.

Gail hoped she would be spared the embarrassment of serving, but her turn came with two minutes left to play in the first half.

"Down their throats, Gail!" O.T. yelled.

She hit the ball high and soft, but at least it went into the right court. Noreen went to the front row to return it.

"We got a point on my serve," Gail said in disbelief. She couldn't resist a little victory hop.

Encouraged, she sent her second serve across the net lower and harder. Noreen set up the return for Margie, who slammed the ball between the opposing players.

The third serve barely cleared the net, but it dropped untouched.

Jubilant, Gail served with confidence. It sailed over the net, but a tall girl on the other team leapt up and hit a spike not even Noreen could return.

"Want to play the other half?" Noreen asked Gail as the official called for them to change courts.

Gail debated a moment, but she feared she'd not equal what she'd done in the first half. "I think I better quit while I'm ahead." She trotted over to stand with the boys and cheer the Raiders as they won by six points.

After the game as the girls were washing up, Margie said, "Noreen, I owe you an apology for laughing at the idea of you bein' a teacher. You sure taught Gail good."

For once Noreen didn't have a reply ready. After a long moment she said, "She learns fast."

"Gail does okay with the boys, too," teased a teammate. "Even Phil cheered when she served those points."

Margie laughed. "I'll bet Veronica and Linda are fit to be tied. Half the boys in our homeroom came to watch us win without those hoity-toities."

"Forget them," Gail said. "I have every class with Veronica. Let me escape her during my lunch hour."

Noreen ran a comb through her dark hair. "Right. Ready to go to study hall?"

"Sure." Gail was pleasantly surprised. Usually Noreen walked off by herself. As they stepped into the hallway, Gail

Chapter Fifteen

said, "Thanks for making me look good in the game."

"You played about ten times better than in the first game." She grinned. "Red must have inspired you. He's cute, and he seems real nice."

"He is." Gail could hardly believe she was talking to Noreen as easily as she would to Alice. "How about your boyfriend? I was so busy looking at the convertible I forgot to look at him until it was too late."

"I'll show you his picture. The car, unfortunately, belongs to his brother. He was drafted this summer, so Kenny's driving it while he's in training at Fort Leonard Wood."

When they reached their assigned table in the library, Gail made her usual fast inspection of the chairs.

Noreen pulled several photos from her billfold. "Here he is."

The black-and-white photo was one of those taken at school. Gail choked back a comment on how old Kenny looked. "He's cute, and he looks like a lot of fun."

"I like him more than anybody I ever dated." Noreen ran her fingers lightly over the photo.

Gail wondered how many boys Noreen could have dated at fourteen. "Are those all pictures of boyfriends?"

"No, worst luck." Noreen held up a photo of a sailor and a young woman with Noreen's face but short hair. "That's my sister and her husband." She shuffled to a photo of a baby. "This is my niece Debbie. I went out to San Diego and helped my sister for three weeks when she was born. I wanted to stay, but I couldn't leave my dad alone."

"Debbie's really sweet." Gail was ashamed at how relieved she was to hear that she hadn't been wrong in defending Noreen.

When the bell rang, both girls went to the stacks to choose a novel. Gail had always read any of the few books she could get her hands on, but she'd never had anyone to talk to about what she read. Going down the shelves with Noreen was a new pleasure. When the librarian shushed them, Gail settled on *The Grapes of Wrath* and moved on to look for books on the Bill of Rights. She needed to come up with something interesting to say about the Ninth and Tenth Amendments.

She spent the rest of the period listing rights taken for granted but not actually written down and powers the states held only because of history and tradition. By the time the bell rang, she still hadn't found a central theme to tie together her bundle of ideas.

She had a huge armload of books to carry home after school. Red took them from her as they walked out to the bus, and she thought how much better her little world looked now than it had the first week of school.

As soon as they sat down on the bus, he said, "What was that malarkey you gave me this morning about what a bad volleyball player you are?"

"That was the best I ever played. Noreen's been coachin'—coaching—me."

Chapter Fifteen

"She plays great, and she must be smart or she wouldn't be on that radio panel." He frowned. "What gets me is that she always acts like she couldn't care less if somebody on fire rolled past her."

Gail couldn't argue about that. "She does go her own way."

He looked at his feet. "I've heard stories about her. Some of the guys say she's pretty fast, necks with high school boys and stuff like that."

Gail guessed the stories combined a little truth and a lot of lies. "They're just jealous because her boyfriend drives a convertible."

Red didn't meet her eyes. "I—I don't know."

Gail's anger began to rise. "The stories aren't true. I've heard them, and I think Veronica and her crowd just made them up to spice up those awful slam books."

"But if even *some* of the stories are true—"

"I won't believe nasty gossip about her." Her anger and her voice rose with every word. She stopped herself. The gossip wasn't Red's fault. "Noreen's been a really great volleyball captain. She helped me when she didn't have to. I think she's swell."

"Okay, okay." Red stared at her a long moment. "I like that you stick up for your friends. I hope she'll be as good a friend to you."

Uncertainty replaced anger. "I don't reckon she trusts anybody very much. She acts like she's older than the rest of us, and she doesn't seem to have any close friends. But I'll be a friend to her anyway."

When the radio panel gathered in Mrs. Ransler's little storage-room office Wednesday afternoon, Veronica took one chair and Noreen the other. She didn't look at Gail, who perched on the table in front of the piles of books and papers. Gail sensed that Noreen didn't want to show Veronica they were friends.

Ralph didn't share that feeling. He perched on the edge of the table with his long legs reaching to the floor and smiled warmly at Gail.

She smiled back, guessing that Red had prompted Ralph's new friendliness.

"The meeting is called to order," Veronica announced. "Unless someone has had a sensational idea for the whole thing, let's just hear what you've come up with."

"Great idea," Arthur said. He sat on the radiator under the window.

Gail wondered whether he had a crush on Veronica—fat chance he'd have against Phil—or just wanted to get in good with the person in power.

"I have the first two amendments, so I'll start," Veronica said.

Listening to the report, Gail regretfully admitted that Veronica was no dumb blonde. As the others gave equally good reports, Gail's confidence plummeted. When her turn

Chapter Fifteen

came, her ideas seemed childish. She stammered when she started, and Ralph smiled encouragement. She glanced at Arthur as she made her first point. Veronica's toady nodded thoughtfully.

Relieved, Gail looked at Noreen for a sign of approval. She was filing her fingernails, but Gail knew her well enough by now to know she was listening, not bored. Gail went on with new confidence.

Veronica's face remained neutral while Gail spoke. "Okay. We all have the facts, but I don't see how we can go on the air with just facts."

"Right," Gail said, glad to agree with Veronica on something. "We need a theme, something to give it all meaning in the middle of the twentieth century."

Ralph nodded. "Only our parents will listen if we don't think of an angle. The Bill of Rights aren't, uh, isn't, news to anybody."

"Maybe that's the problem," Gail said. "We take them so for granted that we forget about our responsibilities in protecting them."

Ralph stood up. "Hey! That's it! We can talk about the average citizen's responsibilities for preserving each amendment."

Arthur nodded. "A Bill of Responsibilities. We could do that in half an hour. What do you think, Veronica?"

"It's corny."

Ralph turned to Noreen. "We haven't heard from you

yet."

"Do what you want. I'll do my share."

Veronica frowned. "People don't want to hear ninth graders preaching about responsibilities. The idea is all wet."

Annoyed, Gail snapped, "Do you have a better one?"

"Almost anything would be better." Veronica glared at her. "I would be ashamed to be chairman of a panel on that."

For a moment no one spoke. Then Ralph said slowly, "This is a democracy. Let's vote on the Bill of Responsibilities theme."

Veronica's light-skinned cheeks turned pink. "All in favor," she muttered.

Ralph and Gail raised their hands. Noreen looked out the window. Arthur scratched his nose.

"We have to report to Mrs. Ransler in five minutes," Ralph said to Arthur. "You know what she said. Either we pull it together or she calls it off."

Slowly Arthur raised his hand.

Ralph turned to Veronica. "That's a majority."

Veronica's face went from pink to rose. "I won't lead a panel with such a lame-brained idea."

The others stared at her in silence.

Arthur cleared his throat but said nothing.

Finally Gail said, "Fine, if that's the way you want it. It was Ralph's idea. He should take the credit or blame for it."

"I'm willing," Ralph said.

Gail shivered at the look of hatred Veronica turned on

Chapter Fifteen

her.

Veronica's face and neck had gone red. "Fine, if that's the way the group wants it. I resign. Let Ralph be chairman."

Arthur leaned forward. "Come on, Veronica, don't be mad. We elected you chairman and we want you to stay chairman. Our vote wasn't against you."

She stood up, her face now confident. "Then change the stupid theme. Otherwise, count me out."

Arthur jammed his hands in his pockets and looked at Ralph and Gail. "We can come up with something we all like."

Mrs. Ransler opened the door. "Ready to report?"

Everyone looked at Veronica.

"I—that is—some of us voted to use a Bill of Responsibilities theme, but not everyone thinks that's a good idea."

Gail added, "We'd talk about the responsibilities that come with rights."

Arthur held up his hand as though he were in a class. "How does that sound, Mrs. Ransler?"

"Promising, but the decision is up to you. Perhaps you should take another vote."

Veronica croaked out, "All in favor."

Ralph, Gail, and then Arthur raised their hands.

Mrs. Ransler smiled. "I'm glad that's settled. When would the chairman like to hold the first rehearsal?"

"Ask Ralph," Veronica said. "I've resigned."

The bell rang, and the five students rushed out of the

room before Mrs. Ransler could ask questions.

"Don't you ever take sides?" Gail asked Noreen as they hurried toward their lockers.

"Why should I? It just causes problems."

"But when you don't vote or say anything, you're letting Veronica do whatever she wants. This radio panel is all about our rights and sticking up for them."

Noreen stopped. "Geez, kid!" She lowered her voice. "Forget about your so-called rights! You just got yourself in big trouble back there. Veronica was nasty to you on general principles when school started, but now she despises you. You should've known better than to take away one of her toys."

"What do you mean?"

Noreen shook her head. "Sometimes you're so naive you're just plain dumb. She had no intention of giving up being chairman. That's prestige. When you took her up on it, she had to resign."

"But I didn't make her! She did it herself."

"That's not the way she sees it. Think about it. You humiliated her by taking away something she wanted. She'll go after you now like a cat after a rat. Believe me, I know."

Chapter Sixteen

Noreen's warning worried Gail so much that she told Red about it on the bus.

He brushed it off. "What could Veronica do to you?"

"I don't know." Gail thought of Veronica's conversation with Linda in Stella's Style Shop. That still stung too much to repeat to Red. "I know she and her friends have done stuff to Noreen—told stories about her, tried to keep her from being volleyball captain, written slams."

"So what does Veronica have against Noreen?"

Gail shrugged. "Maybe Veronica sees Noreen as a rival. Maybe it's just that she's different from the other kids. She seems older and sorta sophisticated." Gail couldn't think of any real reason for Veronica's animosity. "Do you think maybe Veronica's just plain mean? That she just gets a kick out of picking on people?"

"I don't know. We've had a coupla bulls that Pop said were born mean. He never went near them without a pitchfork. People are a lot more complicated than bulls, though. I think they learn to be good or bad."

"Well, I wish somebody would start teaching Veronica to be good. If she tries to push me around, I'm pushing right back. I'm not going to ignore her shenanigans the way Noreen does."

Despite the brave words, Gail's stomach flip-flopped at the thought of Veronica and Linda plotting revenge. But as the day went by, she realized that they, and the rest of Veronica's gang, simply turned or moved away whenever she happened to come near. That suited Gail fine.

When the bell rang at the end of fifth period on Friday and the ninth graders headed for the class meeting in the girls' gym, Gail congratulated herself on having a Veronica-free week.

Noreen brushed past Gail heading away from the gym.

"Noreen, where are you going?"

"I'm cutting out. The election is fixed anyway. Whatever the nomination committee says, goes. See you on Monday."

Gail turned to Margie. "Won't we have any say on candidates?"

"Yes and no. You can nominate from the floor, but nobody bothers. Here's the way it works. Phil and his friends decide who they want and then talk some sacrificial lambs into running against them. That way they can say we had a

Chapter Sixteen

choice."

"Gee whiz! Some democracy this is. Why does everybody let this little clique get away with it?"

"Nobody cares, or at least not enough to do anything about it. The class officers don't really do anything anyway. I'd sneak out myself if I dared."

They took seats in the back row of battered folding chairs as Phil called the meeting to order. He looked poised and confident, and his voice, already a baritone, carried through the gym. "Mrs. Ransler has an announcement before we start."

The teacher's pleasant face was grim. "Today President Truman announced that the Soviet Union has exploded an atomic bomb."

Her tone worried Gail more than her words.

The teacher looked around the gym. "This changes the balance of power in the world, and it may well change your lives. Please pay attention to the news this weekend, not only to the reports on the bomb but also to the government the communists are now forming in China. Monday every social studies class will discuss the threat communism poses to the Free World."

Gail relaxed, thinking Mrs. Ransler just wanted to make sure they paid attention to current events rather than think only about what was happening right here, right now.

Phil stepped back to the front. "The only business we have is nominations for our class elections next Friday." He glanced down at a sheet of paper. "The candidates will make speeches during fourth period, and we'll vote by secret ballot in our homerooms right after that. A special committee will count the ballots in Mr. Addison's office. Arthur, give us the nominating committee's report."

Arthur rose from a front-row seat and faced the class. He stood a foot shorter than Phil and sounded far less confident. "The nominations for secretary are Linda Lester and Wanda Ruckles."

"See," Margie whispered to Gail under the cover of light applause, "Linda's a cinch. Veronica will tell everybody to vote for her buddy. Wanda's such a mouse she'll never get up the nerve to ask anybody to vote for her."

Gail didn't doubt Margie was right. "We have algebra together, and she never says peep."

Arthur shuffled note cards. "The candidates for vice-president are Phil Harvey and Ralph Toffani."

Gail sighed. Ralph wouldn't be a pushover for anybody, but he didn't stand a chance against the school's star athlete.

"The candidate for president is," Arthur paused, "Veronica Holt."

Gail swallowed a groan.

In front of her O.T. bobbed up. "Mr. President, how come we got only one candidate for president?"

Phil smiled. "Nobody is willing to run against Veronica."

Arthur nodded. "We asked three girls, and they all said no."

Ralph stood. "Our class by-laws say we have to

Chapter Sixteen

nominate at least two candidates for each office."

Phil's smile never faded. "The Chair stands ready to receive nominations from the floor."

A buzz went around the room, but no one rose.

Phil called for order. "Do I hear a motion to suspend the rule requiring two nominees?"

O.T. popped up again. "I nominate Janie Wheeler."

"No," Janie sang out. "I don't want to run."

"Smart girl," Gail whispered to Margie.

"Sorry, Janie," Phil said. "If someone seconds your nomination, you're the candidate. Anybody?"

No one spoke.

O.T. tried again. "I nominate Rita Ashbrenner."

Phil called for a second.

"No, please," the girl said. "I already said no."

"Come on, you girls," O.T. pleaded. "Are you all chicken?"

Phil frowned. "You're out of order, O.T. If there are no more nominations, the Chair—"

"Mr. President," O.T. yelled, "I know somebody with the guts to run. I nominate Gail Albright."

As Gail gasped in surprise, two voices called, "I second it."

Phil grinned. "Gail Albright has been nominated. Meeting adjourned."

Chapter Seventeen

Hand waving frantically, Gail tried to protest, but Phil had sprinted for the door and everyone else was getting up.

She buried her face in her hands. "Darn that O.T.! I ought to knock his silly block off for getting me into this mess!"

Red wriggled his way through the crowd. "Congratulations," he said, his face triumphant.

Gail glared at him. "Did you second that nomination?"

"Sure, and so did some girl." His smile faded. "Gail, we can't just roll over and let that bunch have everything their own way."

Ralph pushed his way through, his hand extended. "Glad to share the ticket with you, Gail. We'll put up a real fight."

Gail thought of Noreen's warning. "Ralph, you know

Chapter Seventeen

we don't have a ghost of a chance."

"Heck, no," Ralph agreed. "But we can force them to promise to do something besides plan class parties for their own crowd. We have to go to class now, but I'll talk to you Monday."

Gail forced herself to smile, stand up, and walk with Red to social studies. Her brain had gone numb, and she wanted to kill O.T. for giving Veronica a new way to humiliate her.

He met Gail at the classroom door, his smile big but his voice anxious. "I'll be your campaign manager. You won't need to do much."

She gave him a look that would have sent Bobby running for the nearest tree. "I don't intend to do *anything*."

Veronica smirked. "But Gail, running for office is your responsibility as a citizen. You owe it to your classmates to do your best. As you always say, with rights come responsibilities."

Linda snickered.

Anger heated Gail like a wood stove on a hot day. They were so sure they'd found their chance to stomp on her. If she fought back, they would. But if she didn't do her best, Veronica would win the way she usually did. Promising herself to wipe away their smirks, she corralled her temper and said quietly, "You're right, Veronica. We get the government we deserve. O.T., get busy."

"Hotdog!" His smile was real now. "I knew we could count on you to put up a fight."

"A losing one," Gail said under her breath as she slipped into her seat. For the moment, she didn't care. She looked forward to an open battle against Veronica.

Mrs. Ransler signaled for quiet. She looked at the empty seat next to Gail. "Where's Noreen? She was here this morning. Have you seen her, Gail?"

Gail couldn't lie, but she couldn't say Noreen had sneaked out. "Uh—I didn't see her after the meeting."

Veronica laughed. "You didn't see her *in* the meeting either."

Mrs. Ransler didn't seem to have heard. "We really don't have time left for the assigned lesson, and I don't know enough about the Russian A-bomb test to discuss it. Instead let's talk about elections. Our ninth-grade election is a lesson in itself. I'm very pleased that my students are taking an active role in student government. Class elections give you experience that will be invaluable to you, and to society, the rest of your lives."

She opened the top drawer of her desk and took out a newspaper. "I was disturbed to hear several students say that voting is a waste of time, that the results are completely predictable. I want to remind you of the lesson of our 1948 presidential election." She opened the newspaper so the students could see the front-page headline, "Truman Wins Presidency," and a photo of the triumphant Missourian holding up a newspaper bearing the headline "Dewey Defeats Truman."

She walked across the front of the room so everyone

Chapter Seventeen

could see. "You have six outstanding candidates to choose from, and I'm sure they will conduct thoughtful, imaginative, fair campaigns. And that's all I will say about the election."

O.T. leaned toward Gail and whispered, "I wish she could vote."

Gail could hardly breathe. Mrs. Ransler had made the campaign sound like a big deal, and Gail had no idea what one involved. She faced being humiliated far more than when she'd fallen in the mud and when opposing volleyball teams had zeroed in on her as the weakest player. Once again she wanted to throttle O.T. She turned to glare at him, but he was too busy scribbling notes to notice.

When the bell rang, he grinned at her. "Don't worry. It'll be fun."

Maybe for him, she thought, as she gathered her books and went to meet the bus. She was pleasantly surprised when Mr. Wilkins and several kids congratulated her, and the junior high kids on her bus all gave her a big cheer as she sat down by Red. Since everyone expected her to be happy and proud, she tried to fake a confidence she didn't feel.

Alice leaned forward in her window seat to talk across Pete. "I didn't know that Linda is a friend of yours."

"The skinny Linda who follows Veronica around? She's not."

"But she must be," Alice said. "She seconded your nomination."

Gail felt as though someone had punched her in the

stomach. "She liked the idea of Veronica running against someone so easy to beat."

Everyone sat silent as the truth of Gail's remark sank in.

Pete recovered first. "You won't get skunked. All the country kids will vote for you."

"And the girls on your volleyball team," Alice added.

Gail sighed. "That gives me about thirty votes to Veronica's ninety."

"So get more," Red urged her. "We're not the only ones who think Veronica's a snot. You just have to give the town kids a good reason to vote for you instead of her."

Red's support pleased and encouraged Gail. "Yeah, maybe have a campaign platform like the Republicans and the Democrats did in the presidential election."

"Right." Red's face had lost its grimness. "Ralph has some good ideas. That's why he agreed to run. He knows he can't beat a popular guy like Phil, but he's sick and tired of that clique running everything."

Gail perked up. Even if she couldn't win, she could come up with some good ideas and stand up to Veronica. "I guess the speeches are to tell everybody what we support, what we want to change." She thought a moment. "I'd sure like to change the activities we can sign up for at noon. I'll make some notes this weekend. I'd appreciate it if you'd all think about it, too."

* * *

Chapter Seventeen

As it turned out, she had little time to think about anything that weekend. Friday evening she helped her mother milk the cows while her father covered baled hay stacked in the barn lot with tarpaulins in preparation for a predicted storm. Saturday morning he called her and Bobby out of bed to help drive their dairy cows out of the cornfield and mend the broken fence so they couldn't get back in.

As the Albrights got ready to go to town that night to buy groceries and Gail's winter coat, Ratter began barking wildly near the henhouse. Her father grabbed the rifle that hung over the kitchen door, vowing to shoot the raccoon that had been raiding the chickens. Gail followed him with a flashlight, and together they trailed the dog around the farm on a futile coon hunt for two hours. After that they staked out the henhouse until rain drove them back indoors.

Sunday afternoon as Gail drowsed over her algebra, her father shouted that the wind was picking up and he needed everyone to help him tack down the canvas tarpaulins that were blowing off the bales. By the time the family came back to the house drenched through, the wind was blowing so hard that it tore a couple of dozen shingles off the henhouse. As soon as the storm passed, Gail and her father armed themselves with hammers and nails and went out to repair the damage.

Sunday evening, before the family sat down to a quick supper of fried potatoes mixed with eggs and bacon, Gail put two big buckets of bath water on the wood stove to heat. After supper she bathed in the round tin tub that seemed to shrink as she grew. Her mother insisted she go to bed as soon as she finished her algebra.

The first thing Gail saw when she stepped into the school Monday morning was a big yellow poster that said in blue letters, "A Vote for Veronica Is a Vote for Victory."

A few feet down the hall another yellow poster said, "Vote for Experience: Veronica, Phil, Linda."

By the door of homeroom a yellow poster had a giant blue V as the first letter for three words: "Vote Veronica Victory."

Ralph and O.T. met her at the door.

O.T. skipped the greeting. "We've got to get busy. They've got posters all over the school."

Gail felt sick. She had no poster paper or paint —or money to buy them. "I had no idea we'd need posters. I thought we'd just make speeches on Friday."

The warning bell rang.

Ralph headed out the door, calling over his shoulder, "We need to make plans. We're meeting just outside the front door at noon."

O.T. looked past Gail. "Hi, Noreen. Who are you going to vote for?"

Noreen put her books on the shelf under her chair and opened a *Saturday Evening Post*. "You know I never vote."

O.T. frowned. "Not even for Gail?"

Noreen closed her magazine. "What in heck

Chapter Seventeen

happened Friday?"

Despair flooded through Gail. "This idiot nominated me for class president."

Noreen muttered something and opened her magazine. "That's so dumb I don't want to hear one word about it all week."

Gail's misery deepened. She hadn't expected congratulations, but she'd thought Noreen would say something encouraging, or at least sympathize.

O.T. reached across Gail and grabbed Noreen's magazine. "Some friend you are. You really go out of your way to repay somebody who's helped you."

Gail jerked the magazine out of his hand. "Noreen doesn't owe me a darn thing. Mind your own business, for a change."

Noreen took the magazine, turned a page, and reached in her purse for a pencil. Her hands tightened around it.

Anticipating another broken pencil, Gail held out her hand. "Noreen, can I borrow your pencil, please?"

"Sure." She handed it to Gail without looking up.

The bell rang, and Noreen reached into her purse and pulled out the top half of a broken pencil. "Ouch!"

Mrs. Ransler stepped toward her. "What's the matter, Noreen?"

"I just ran a splinter in my hand."

Mrs. Ransler walked back to her desk. "I have a needle for just such emergencies."

Gail reached for the needle the teacher offered. "Let me get it out for you."

"I can do it."

Gail handed the needle to Noreen, watched her struggle for a few seconds, and opened the algebra book to recheck a problem. When Gail finished, Noreen was glowering at the splinter still deep in the palm of her right hand. Gail started to offer to help again, but she stopped herself. Noreen needed to realize that you have to accept help sometimes.

Noreen whispered, "I'm not very good with my left hand."

Gail opened her speech textbook. "You're not going to be able to do much with your right hand either if you keep poking it full of holes."

A minute later Noreen elbowed Gail. "Will you get this damn thing out? Please."

Gail closed her book. Getting slivers out was something she knew how to do. She had Noreen's out in a few seconds.

Mrs. Ransler reclaimed her needle. "Funny how much easier that was when Gail did it. We missed you in social studies Friday, Noreen."

"Sorry. I didn't think we'd have time for class after the meeting."

"I'll be taking roll at the next class meeting," the teacher warned.

"Oh, I wouldn't miss that one for anything," Noreen said.

Chapter Seventeen

"Yeah," Gail added as Mrs. Ransler walked away. "You wouldn't want to miss seeing me make a fool of myself, again."

Noreen studied her a moment. "You'll survive, kid."

Gail didn't feel too sure of that as she took her lunch from her locker and went outside at noon. She'd seen at least twenty-five posters that morning, and several classmates had asked when she was putting hers up.

To her surprise, Red was waiting with Ralph, O.T., and Wanda. As students were forbidden to linger in front of the school at noon, they walked down the street to a vacant lot and sat on a fallen tree.

Gail brought out her fried egg sandwich. "How on earth are we going to get stuff to make posters?"

Wanda, a short, chubby girl with frizzy brown hair, opened a spiral notebook. "I can get everything we need after school today."

"You'll need slogans to put on 'em," Red said, unwrapping the waxed paper around two peanut butter sandwiches made with thick slices of homemade bread. "Ralph has a coupla good ideas."

Ralph nodded. "If we can come up with a few, O.T., Wanda, and I can work on them at my house tonight."

O.T. bounced up and began to pace. "Good. I think Mrs. Ransler and Mr. Wilkins will let us out of homeroom to put them up."

Wanda took notes as the group agreed that they should

campaign together but feature Gail as the leader of the ticket. By the time they headed back to school, they had chosen black on orange as their colors and written four simple slogans.

Although Gail felt guilty that she couldn't pay for any of the materials, she enjoyed the same sense of belonging she had with the volleyball team.

During gym class that afternoon, Margie and two other Raiders offered to help make posters, but Noreen remained silent. She didn't coach Gail on her serve and walked off to the next class alone.

Gail couldn't figure out whether Noreen was angry, disappointed, or just didn't want to be associated with someone so dead center in Veronica's sights.

When Gail walked into social studies sixth period, Noreen was holding half a broken pencil in each fist.

"I know why you borrowed my pencil this morning," she said as Gail sat down.

Gail knew she was supposed to say something, but what? "Is—is something wrong?"

Noreen opened a *Collier's*. "Everything is just peachy."

Mrs. Ransler called for quiet and came to stand in front of Noreen. "I'd bawl you out for reading a magazine in class, if I thought you could read upside down."

A blush spread up Noreen's usually imperturbable face, and her right hand clenched the top half of the pencil.

Chapter Seventeen

The class watched in complete silence.

Gail heard herself say, "Noreen isn't feeling very well today."

Mrs. Ransler touched Noreen's forehead. "You are a little flushed. Would you like to go on home?"

Noreen stared at her desk, saying nothing.

O.T. raised his hand. "This is the nurse's afternoon in the health office."

Mrs. Ransler studied Noreen a moment. "Gail, go with Noreen to the nurse, please."

Gail didn't want to face Noreen's anger in the hall alone, but she couldn't back out. She grabbed her purse and headed for the door. She was relieved when she heard Noreen behind her.

Noreen waited until they were well out of earshot. "What's wrong with you? Why did you tell her I'm sick?"

Gail kept moving. "I don't know." That wouldn't satisfy Noreen, and Gail couldn't say she wanted to protect her. She settled on a half-truth. "You've been acting kinda funny all day, breaking pencils and stuff. I thought maybe you are sick."

"Well, I'm not. What am I going to tell the nurse?"

Gail hadn't thought that far ahead. She envisioned another visit to Addison's office and groaned. "I'm sorry. It was stupid of me."

"I'll ask her about my hand," Noreen said, ignoring Gail's apology.

The nurse was so impressed with the hole in Noreen's

palm that she gave her a tetanus shot.

"Now I am sick," Noreen said as they walked back to class. "My arm hurts like hell."

"You'll survive."

Noreen grinned. "I'm pretty tough, all right."

Gail doubted that. "If you're so tough, why do you back off from trouble so fast?"

"I don't back off when it's worth the effort, when it really matters."

"What's worth it?"

Noreen looked away. "Not much around here."

Mrs. Ransler raised a questioning eyebrow as they came back into class.

"She got a shot," Gail said, and scolded herself for interfering again.

She realized what a poor job she'd done of covering up when she and Red took their seat on the bus.

"What was with Noreen today?" Red asked. "She's not the type to get upset because a teacher says something to her. And don't tell me she was sick."

Gail shrugged. If she hadn't fooled Red, she certainly hadn't fooled Mrs. Ransler, but the teacher seemed to have a soft spot for Noreen. "Something was bothering her all day. Maybe she had a fight with her boyfriend."

The next morning Gail rushed to homeroom as soon as the bus dropped the students off. Margie and O.T. were

Chapter Seventeen

working on posters in Mrs. Ransler's storage room.

Gail's spirits lifted as she read, "Go With Gail," "Run With Ralph," "Win With Wanda," and her favorite, "Vote for Yourself! Vote, Gail, Wanda, Ralph!"

"We didn't finish all of them last night," O.T. told Gail. "Keep painting while I start putting them up." He stuck his head out the door. "Hey, Noreen, we could use an extra artist here."

"I'll help," one of the Raiders said, but Noreen didn't look up from her magazine.

"Takes dynamite to move Noreen," O.T. said. "She didn't used to be that way." He rushed out carrying several posters.

Gail took a brush, dipped it in a bottle of India ink, and filled in the letters already penciled on the paper. She was relieved to be actually doing something.

Walking through the halls later that morning, she began to hope that the election could become a real race.

The candidates, O.T., and Red met for lunch at the tree to discuss the speeches at the class meeting on Friday. Wanda and Ralph both had definite ideas about changes the class officers should make, and Gail's respect for them grew. They had so much to say they didn't get back to the school until the warning bell was ringing.

"Hold it!" O.T said as they rushed in the door. "I put a 'Go With Gail' right there this morning."

They stood in front of a yellow poster and read:

The Feedsack Dress

Veronica Victory.

Gail A Big Wind.

Chapter Eighteen

O.T. ran down the hall. "They've torn down all our posters and put up their own!"

"That's dirty!" Ralph fumed. "I'm going to tell the principal!"

Gail reacted without thinking: "No! We'll handle this ourselves."

"She's right," Red said. "You'll seem like babies if you run to the principal. What'll we do, Gail?"

She had no idea, but with everyone looking at her, she had to come up with something. "First, we need to make new posters. Where can we get more paper?"

No one spoke.

Heart pounding at her daring, Gail reached up and loosened the tape holding up Veronica's poster. "We'll use their yellow paper but letter in black and make our posters horizontal instead of vertical."

Red nodded. "And glue them to the wall."

O.T. moved down the nearly empty hall. "Everybody collect posters."

"Just the ones that replaced ours, please," Wanda said, her voice anxious. "I wouldn't feel right about taking the others."

O.T. jerked down a poster. "Good idea. If they complain about it, they'll have to admit they tore ours down."

"Yeah," Gail said. "I think Miss Watson will let Margie and me work on them in study hall if we keep quiet."

Wanda stood straighter. "I'm on my way to art class. I'll get paint and brushes and ask to be excused to work on the posters. After all, that's an art project."

Ralph paused to retrieve a poster. "I'll ask Mr. Wilkins to excuse me and Red to do some work on our 'science project' in the library." He rolled up the poster and handed it to Gail. "See you there in about ten minutes, I hope."

Gail reached study hall just as the last bell rang.

"Where have you been?" Noreen demanded. "What are you going to do about this?" She held up a yellow poster.

The line at the top read, "Veronica Has Verve." A sketch of a long-haired girl wearing a party dress obviously portrayed Veronica. The bottom half of the poster showed a scarecrow wearing a sack with a morning glory pattern. Below it were the words "Gail Has Gall."

Gail reddened with embarrassment. Once again the

Chapter Eighteen

hated feedsack dress was labeling her a hick. Another thought struck her. It was dumb of Veronica to attack in this small, mean way. Lots of the kids wouldn't like it. "Where did you get this?"

"The girls' restroom. Those jackasses have stolen all your posters and put up garbage like this. We've got to wreck their little red wagon!"

Gail couldn't believe her ears. "*We?*"

Noreen tossed Gail's books onto the neighboring table. "I got Miss Watson's permission for us to make posters."

Gail could hardly keep from laughing at Noreen's conversion from passivist to activist. "I don't know," she said, pretending despair. "I think I better just forget the whole thing. It's so hopeless. Let them do what they want."

Noreen patted her on the shoulder. "Don't get discouraged, kid. We'll all help you. Veronica's not going to get away with it this time."

"You've convinced me," Gail said, unable to keep from grinning.

"It's nothing to laugh about," Noreen scolded. "She thinks she can run everything and ruin anybody. Maybe if I hadn't ignored her badmouthing last year, she wouldn't be so cock-eyed sure she can get by with it now. It just seemed so— so silly compared to, well, real problems."

Gail knew Noreen meant losing her mother and other family problems. "Why did Veronica do that to you?"

"She was jealous because Phil was making eyes at

me."

The librarian started toward their table, but Noreen didn't notice. "You can't let Veronica walk over you, Gail. You've got to defend yourself." She took a deep breath. "No, defense won't do it. We've got to attack!"

Alarmed by Noreen's anger and her loud expression of it, Gail eased her friend into a chair and whispered, "We will. Here comes our work crew now."

O.T., Ralph, and Red, all smiling, plopped a pile of yellow posters down in front of Noreen.

Wanda put bottles of India ink and half a dozen brushes by the paper and whispered, "Welcome to the campaign, Noreen."

Frowning, Miss Watson approached the table. "Noreen, I won't warn you again. You can work here only if you are *quiet.*"

They all nodded and remained silent as she walked away.

Noreen picked up a brush and whispered. "You can't fight poison with pablum. We got to come up with some real shots. And some good reasons to vote for Gail."

Gail nodded. "We need a platform *now*. We can't wait until our speeches."

Wanda spread out cutouts of the letters they had used in sketching the letters for the earlier posters. "If we write it this afternoon, I can type up a ditto master and mimeograph it tonight at the church before the youth group meets. We can crank out enough copies to pass out to everyone

Chapter Eighteen

tomorrow in the homerooms."

"Go ahead, candidates," Noreen said. "You write the platform while the rest of us make posters."

Worried about what Noreen might put on them, Gail hesitated. She looked at Red.

He winked. "I'll help with the posters."

Gail, Ralph, and Wanda went to an empty table in the corner.

Ralph cleaned his glasses with a handkerchief. "Boy, this isn't going to be easy. It's just like that radio panel. We've got a bunch of ideas and nothing to hold them together. We need a theme."

Ralph's mention of the radio show gave Gail an idea. "Students' rights. We'll write our platform as the Students' Bill of Rights."

Wanda wrote a number one on a sheet of paper. "What comes first?"

Looking at her fellow campaigners, Gail decided the nominating committee hadn't been so smart in picking its patsies after all.

All three agreed immediately that they wanted the choice of extracurricular activities changed and that most of the other students did, too. Although Ralph and Wanda both walked home for lunch, they sympathized with the plight of the students who ate in the Jail. The three discussed a dozen other possibilities but, with five minutes left in the period, decided on seven.

They were still working on the draft when Noreen came over to them. "It's a minute or so until the bell. Come see the new posters and take a couple to hang up on your way to class."

Ralph stood. "Why don't you polish the draft in social studies, Gail?"

"Right, and I'll pass it on to Wanda after school," Gail said as they moved over to the poster table.

"Noreen made up some dandy slogans," O.T. said with a wide grin, "but we were afraid to use them."

"I like 'Albright Is For All' best," Red said, holding one up.

The other new ones said, "To Put Things Right, Elect Gail Albright" and "Albright's for All Students' Rights."

Gail was disappointed that the slogans didn't have more punch. Then she noticed a bigger problem. "Where are the posters for Ralph and Wanda? These are all for me."

Noreen and Red looked at each other, their faces guilty.

O.T. picked up a pile of posters. "These are just the new slogans. We already 'went to the restroom' and put up a dozen posters with the old slogans."

Ralph smiled as he took two of the posters. "Next time I'll have *my* friends make the posters."

Wanda shrugged. "We'll all win or we'll all lose. Gail is the one Veronica's going after, so she's the one we should campaign for the hardest."

* * *

Chapter Eighteen

Gail could think of nothing but the Students' Bill of Rights during fifth period, but she didn't dare risk annoying the teacher by looking at the draft until she went into social studies. Mrs. Ransler paused in front of Gail long enough to look at the paper and then ignored it as Gail, Noreen, and O.T. passed the sheet back and forth and polished it during class discussion. To show she was paying attention, Gail volunteered answers to two of Mrs. Ransler's questions while copying the final draft to show Red on the bus.

As soon as he'd read it, he insisted on standing and reading it aloud to the whole bus. "We, the candidates of the Students' Rights Party, pledge ourselves to work for the adoption of the following Students' Bill of Rights.

"One: Students shall have the right to peaceable assembly in the school and on school grounds during lunch hour and one-half hour before and after school."

"I'm for that," Alice said. "I hate staying in Jail the whole noon hour."

"Two: No students shall be required to participate in extracurricular activities; all activities shall be open to all students."

One of the boys yelled, "Down with Personal Grooming at noon."

"Three: Students shall have the right to petition the school administration to change rules that are unfair or outdated."

The bus lurched, and Pete and Gail grabbed Red to

steady him.

"Four: All classes, including industrial arts and home economics, will be open to both boys and girls."

A high school girl clapped. "I begged the principal to let me take wood shop, but he said it wasn't 'suitable for young ladies.'"

"Five: No cruel and unusual punishment may be imposed by teachers or the principal."

Pete grinned. "You mean like an indefinite noon-hour detention?"

Red cleared his throat. "Six: The enumeration of rights above does not deny others retained by the students.

"Seven: The students recognize that all rights must be exercised in a responsible manner."

Several senior high school students shook their heads or laughed. A senior girl said, "Ol' Addison is going to be plenty mad when he sees this."

Red sat down. "She's right, but I sure like it anyway."

Gail refused to let the prospect of the principal's disapproval dampen her spirits. "At least I won't be in trouble alone this time."

"O.T. didn't seem worried," Red said. "After I got past mad and started getting even, I had fun. You shoulda heard the stuff Noreen was saying about Veronica. She makes posters the way she plays volleyball."

"I guess she just had to get mad."

"She was doing it because you're her friend, not just

because she was mad."

"Gail," Alice called from her seat by Pete, "would you like for me to talk to the girls in the Jail for you? I can say things about you that you can't."

"Yes, thanks a lot." Gail was surprised that Alice could get up the nerve to talk to all those kids she barely knew.

"I'll do the same in the boys' Jail," Pete offered.

Gail smiled as she thought how the nasty posters had backfired. Her team had just begun to fight.

When Gail walked into school the next morning, several students she didn't know spoke to her, and half a dozen girls in her homeroom made a point of being friendly.

O.T., Noreen, and Margie hadn't come in yet when the last bell rang, but Mrs. Ransler didn't call for quiet until they slipped into their seats.

She opened her roll book. "Do we have any announcements this morning?"

Noreen handed Gail a stack of slick, smelly ditto papers.

Gail raised her hand. "I have something I'd like to distribute. It's the platform of the Students' Rights Party."

The teacher nodded. "I believe that's in order."

No one read the paper with more interest than the three opposition candidates.

Gail was disappointed that Mrs. Ransler put her copy down on the desk without reading it and filled out the attendance slip. Gail poked Noreen and pointed her chin at the teacher.

Noreen grinned and whispered. "She read it after school yesterday. She said it's idealistic but unrealistic. And she knew about Veronica's slam posters."

O.T. leaned over. "So did Dad, and unrealistic is a big compliment compared to what he said about your platform. But he appointed me to the committee to count ballots anyway."

All morning students asked Gail about her Students' Bill of Rights. She was jubilant at noon as she hurried to the fallen tree she and her fellow campaigners had labeled party headquarters.

Red was pacing back and forth. "Where've you been? Did Addison call you in?"

"No. Kids kept stopping me. Passing out our platform was a really good idea."

Wanda smiled. "Yes. We may have a small chance now. I think the kids will listen to what we have to say Friday."

The group decided Wanda would talk about why they needed a Bill of Rights. Ralph would give the facts about how little Phil had done for the majority of the students as class president and question any promises he made. Gail would review the platform and discuss their most important goals. They agreed to meet at noon Friday for a final rehearsal.

As they ended their meeting and headed back to school, Gail thought how different her life had become in only one month. Her eight years at the one-room school seemed in

Chapter Eighteen

the distant past. Now some days went better than others, but they were all exciting.

When she walked into the locker room to dress for gym, she heard angry voices.

"That Bill of Rights is nothing but crap," Linda said. "Addison is the principal and he makes the rules. Gail Albright doesn't know anything about this school. She's sticking her nose in where she's not wanted."

"We'll see who's not wanted on Friday!" Margie stormed.

"Nobody is going to vote for that ragamuffin," Veronica said, her voice disdainful. "Her students' rights are students' stupidity."

Gail debated whether to stay back or join the battle. Then, deciding to defend herself, she walked around the bank of lockers.

"Veronica," Noreen said mockingly, "will you resign from class if Gail's elected? Like you resigned as chairman of the radio panel when you were outvoted?"

Face contorted, Veronica glared at Noreen. "I hope you keep on campaigning for her because everybody knows what you are, you cheap—"

Gail gasped and stepped toward Veronica, but before Gail could speak, Mrs. Chapelli's voice froze everyone. "Girls! Veronica, apologize to Noreen. *Now!*"

Veronica stared at the teacher a long time before muttering, "I apologize."

Mrs. Chapelli looked around the locker room. "If I hear anything like that from any of you again, the principal will hear about it." She took a deep breath. "Those of you who are dressed, get into the gym and line up. And no talking!"

Everyone but Gail, Noreen, and three other girls left.

Awash with anger, Gail took her gym clothes from the locker and tried to calm down. As soon as the three other girls left, she said, "I think we've got them scared."

Noreen slumped down on a bench, her face pale. "Maybe Veronica is right."

Gail decided to misunderstand. "That they won't elect a ragamuffin?"

"No, I—look, Gail, we know there's guilt by association. Kids hear a lot of stories about me and—and boys. I think you'd be better off if I keep out of the campaign from now on."

Even as she realized Noreen might be right, Gail answered, "Don't be silly. Nobody believes those stories, not even the people who spread them in the first place."

Noreen covered her face with her hands. "You're so damn naive. You just don't understand."

"I do understand." Gail sat down by her. "I want you on my team, and I know you'll be a big help." Just saying it didn't make it so. She had to convince Noreen, and herself. "After all, the Raiders elected you captain of the volleyball team—twice. The girls voted for you, even though it meant playing with a fumble-fingers like me. They didn't give in to

Chapter Eighteen

Linda and Veronica, and we won't either."

Noreen sat a little straighter, but she still didn't meet Gail's eyes.

"Backing out now would be letting Veronica win a round, Noreen. Promise me you won't run out on us."

Noreen's color returned. "Okay. You're right. This is one of those times I'm going to have to tough it out."

"And we'll have fun, too, just like with the volleyball team. Oh, we're going to start making lists of sure votes and possibles. Then we'll talk to the possibles."

"Good idea. I'll give you my list in social studies." Noreen stood up. "Let's go pound some balls."

Gail relaxed. "Ralph says we may have a chance after all."

"Don't get your hopes up, kid. Veronica's not through yet. If she thinks you have a ghost of a chance, she'll come up with another dirty trick."

Chapter Nineteen

The next morning Noreen rushed into homeroom waving a brown autograph book. "Look at this crap," she said, dropping it on top of Gail's open algebra book.

Gail had never owned an autograph book, but she knew people wrote compliments for the owner on the blank pages. Opening it, she soon saw it was a slam book directed at her, Wanda, and Ralph. At first Gail thought the slams too childish and mean-spirited to influence any voters, but her anger built with every page. She blurted, "Bastards" when she came to drawings showing Ralph as a stick-thin Jack Sprat, Wanda as a balloon-like Mrs. Sprat, and Gail as a chicken dressed in a feedsack.

Mrs. Ransler stepped over to her with a frown, jerked the little book from Gail's hands, flipped through it, and beckoned Linda to come forward. They went into the hall.

Chapter Nineteen

"Hotdog!" Noreen said softly. "I'll bet Mrs. Ransler recognized Linda's writing."

Gail glanced back at Veronica. Her head was down, supposedly to study an open book, and her long blonde hair fell over her face.

A minute later Mrs. Ransler returned alone and without the book.

O.T. took a pencil from behind his ear and scrawled to Gail on his notebook. "The P hates slam books. He'll burn it in front of her and give her detention."

Even so, Linda's visit to the office didn't stop the slam books. Gail saw them being passed around in the halls and in classes all morning. At noon she escaped the school to walk the three blocks uptown to buy the winter coat she had tried on at the department store. It was on sale for twenty dollars.

Walking past Stella's Style Shop, she paused to admire the beautiful plaid dress with its subtle mingling of blues and purples. Even on the mannequin, the fashionable, voluminous skirt fell in beautiful soft folds.

"I wouldn't look like Raggedy Ann in that," Gail thought, and her legs carried her into the store.

Two minutes later Stella persuaded Gail to try the dress on. Looking at herself in the store's three-sided mirror, she wanted desperately to be that chic girl when she stood in front of the ninth grade the next day.

"It's perfect for you, dear," Stella said. "It doesn't need any alteration at all. And you have just the right coloring

The Feedsack Dress

for it."

Gail agreed, and for one moment she smiled at the girl in the mirror. Then reality hit. Embarrassed to admit she couldn't possibly afford it, she said, "I don't have enough money with me today."

Stella plucked a loose bit of thread from the shoulder. "I don't usually do this, but this dress looks so nice on you, I'll take off a little. You can have it for twenty-three dollars."

Gail knew that was a good price for the dress, but it still cost more than the new winter coat. Turning around to see how the dress fell in the back, she found it irresistible. She wondered if she could wear the old coat until Christmas. If she saved all her allowance and didn't buy the jeans, she would have half of the money for the coat, and her mother had promised clothes for Christmas.

"I'll take it." The words shocked her, but once they were out, she couldn't take them back.

Stella packed the dress in a special cardboard box so that Gail wouldn't wrinkle it on the way home. As Stella tied a wide white ribbon around the box, Gail tried to say she'd changed her mind. Instead she counted out the money.

Twice on her way back to school Gail almost turned around to take the dress back, but the picture of herself standing triumphantly fashionable in front of the class kept her going. She told herself that her mother would understand how important it was not to look poor in front of all those town kids.

Chapter Nineteen

The glow of her purchase hadn't worn off when she put the box into her locker. Thinking of it as her secret weapon, she decided to say nothing about it to anyone.

Veronica and Phil were whispering and laughing together after social studies that afternoon, and Gail lingered after the bell to talk to Noreen and O.T. about it.

"They're up to no good," Noreen insisted.

O.T. smiled grimly. "It won't be more slam books."

"Gail!" Red shouted from the hall. "Come on. You'll miss the bus."

Gail ran without going to her locker.

Her mother met her at the back door. "Where's the coat?"

Gail thought surely her mother would understand how important the dress was. Intending to tell her everything, Gail replied instead, "I didn't get—get a chance to go to the department store." Shame had stopped her as she realized all her reasons for buying the dress boiled down to vanity and pride. She'd have to take it back. And she'd have to tell her mother what she'd done. But not now when she might cry from humiliation, or from the yearning to wear that beautiful dress.

Her mother had turned away to finish skimming cream from a gallon jar of milk. "Be sure you go tomorrow, Gail. The coat may be gone by the time we get to town Saturday. I got out your old one to see if you can wear it for chores.

The Feedsack Dress

Come try it on."

Gail's wrists stuck out almost two inches, the buttons wouldn't fasten, and she couldn't flex her shoulders. Even her mother couldn't let it out enough that she could wear it to school. Gail tried again to confess that she'd bought the dress, but the words lodged in her throat. She knew that her parents were watching every dime until they sold the corn, and that wouldn't be for at least a month. Her mother would understand Gail's wanting the dress, but Gail couldn't bear to hurt her by explaining about the posters and the slam books and the nasty things Veronica and Linda were saying.

After supper Gail worked on her speech to the class and an explanation to her parents at the same time. Neither went well. She got ready for bed hoping both would come to her in the night.

Her mother came in carrying the feedsack dress. "The weather's going to be warm again tomorrow, sweetheart, so I got your morning glory dress ready. You want to look nice when you give your speech." She smoothed back Gail's hair and kissed her on the cheek. "We're so proud of you."

Gail swallowed a lump in her throat and a chunk of pride. She'd have to wear the darn feedsack to school. "Thanks, Mom."

Walking into school in that dress was one of the hardest things Gail had ever done. All morning she heard snickers and whispered remarks from Linda, Veronica, and

Chapter Nineteen

their friends. When the bell ending the morning rang, she rushed to get out of the building and down to the fallen tree to meet with her fellow candidates and O.T., Noreen, and Red.

Wanda and Ralph rehearsed their speeches first. Gail, afraid hers would let them down, felt her throat tighten. She shuffled the index cards that held her notes and lost her place. The others' prompt, nervous encouragement when she finished told her she'd been right to worry.

Next they went through their lists of supporters, and it fell far short of the sixty-one they needed to win.

"But we're getting close," O.T. said, as everyone stood up to leave. "If you guys really pour it on in your speeches, we just might make it."

Noreen frowned at him. "Jeez, O.T.! That really helps them relax."

Ralph started toward the school and then turned back to say, "We may not win, but we sure stopped the annual blitzkrieg. That makes it worth it."

Although Gail had never expected to win, the thought of losing to Veronica hurt like touching a hot stove. Her steps slowed, and she and Noreen fell behind the others. "You were right. This whole election is just one big humiliation."

"It's too late to turn yellow, kid. When you stand up there today, you've got to look like you own the world."

"That's what I thought yesterday." She took a deep breath. "I went downtown to buy my winter coat. Instead

The Feedsack Dress

I bought a dress at Stella's."

"You don't seem very happy about it."

"Now I have to tell my parents what I did and why. And find a way to get money for the coat I was supposed to buy before the weather turns cold."

"You're in a pickle, all right." Noreen sighed. "I'd lend you some dough if I had it, but I don't have more than a couple of dollars myself."

Gail's cheeks flamed. "I wasn't hinting for you to lend me money, Noreen. I just needed to tell somebody."

After they'd walked a few steps, Noreen said, "Actually, the answer's pretty obvious. You wear the dress to give the speech and then return it to the store."

For a moment Gail was tempted. "Naw, I couldn't do that. It wouldn't be honest. Besides, every girl in the class would know what I did."

"You could be like Scarlett O'Hara—do what you need to do today and worry about it tomorrow." She stopped at the school door. "You go ahead and change. I'll stay here and see if I can land you a couple more votes."

Gail hurried to her locker. As she dropped in her uneaten lunch, a boiled egg rolled out of the paper bag onto the floor. She picked the egg up and put it into the locker.

Linda passed by and sneered, "Lay another egg?"

Biting back a reply, Gail reached for the dress. "I'll fight them on their own level," she murmured to herself. Hand on the box, she stopped. *What am I doing? I don't want*

Chapter Nineteen

to be on their level. And buying this dress was thinking the way they think.

She shoved the box back into her locker, grabbed the cards on which she'd outlined her speech, and slammed the door shut. Rushing to lock away temptation, she didn't notice that the egg had rolled out onto the floor again. She picked it up, but she didn't dare unlock the door separating her from that beautiful dress. She hurried down the hall trying to stuff the egg into her small purse. When she couldn't, she decided to toss it into the first trashcan she came to.

Noreen fell into step beside her. "Where's the new dress?"

"In my locker. I won't let Veronica make me ashamed of being what I am. I'll just have to tell my parents what I did and take the dress back to Stella's tomorrow."

"O.T. was right. You've got guts, but you won't have to tell your parents. Kenny's picking me up after school. He'll give us a ride to Stella's and then to your farm."

"Thanks. Thanks a lot." Relief and gratitude swept through Gail. "Mom would feel so bad if she knew how much I wanted that dress."

Wanda met them at the door of the gym. Her face grim, she pointed to the small speaker's table at the front of the room.

Feedsacks matching Gail's dress formed an apron around the table's front and sides. Big black capital letters stamped on the front spelled out "Holt's Chicken Feed."

Gail stared at it, anger pouring through her body like lava from a volcano.

"Damn Veronica!" Noreen said. "Let's rip that off of there."

Wanda put a restraining hand on her shoulder. "Ralph and Red already tried. Phil and his friends are standing guard."

"Never mind," Gail said. Her anger turned into determination. Pretending a huge hand was pushing her, she walked to the front row and sat down by Ralph.

He studied her face a moment before saying, "O.T. found out that five people are absent today. He says we need fifty-nine votes to win."

She tried to joke. "Only fifty-nine? That's chicken feed." Her mind raced. The speech she'd planned wouldn't do. She knew exactly what she wanted to say about her opponents, and knew she dare not say such things in public. While the candidates for secretary and vice president spoke, she discarded a series of lame ideas and weak opening lines.

Gail forced herself to listen when Veronica took her place at the speaker's table. She had changed from her usual skirt and blouse to a pink and white taffeta dress that made her look like a girl on a valentine card. She spoke well as she pointed out the difficulties in getting approval of the Students' Bill of Rights.

She didn't mention her opponents until her conclusion: "When you vote, remember that the three students

Chapter Nineteen

sponsoring this pie-in-the-sky Bill of Rights have no experience in student government and have never helped organize school social events. The candidate for president has attended this school for only a month and doesn't even know most of you. Being a class officer is a big job, and it takes a lot of time. But she can't stay after school to work with committees or do all the other things the president has to do.

"Phil, Linda, and I offer you the experience and the ability to get things done."

The applause told Gail that Veronica had made a good speech, a better one than Gail had written. With nothing to lose, she had to go all out. Taking a deep breath, she stood and put her purse on the chair. She started to put the egg there, too, but she feared it would roll off and provoke laughter. Concealing it in her right hand, she walked the few steps toward the speaker's table. Determined to attack rather than defend, she stepped in front of rather than behind the table.

A murmur went through the audience as students saw her dress blend into the cloth around the table.

Gail held the hard-boiled egg behind her back. The familiar shape felt soothing. "It looks like my opponents think I belong at the president's table."

A ripple of responsive laughter boosted her confidence.

"I intended to talk to you about the Students' Bill of Rights, but as Veronica said, most of you have been here a lot longer than I have. You know better than I do that we need to make some changes."

She needed her hands to talk, not behind her back, but she didn't dare put the egg on the table. It might roll off. To calm herself, she began to toss the egg from one hand to the other, back and forth over two or three inches of conspicuous space.

"I don't hesitate to ask all of you to vote for Ralph and Wanda. I know, and I'm sure most of you know, they would be outstanding officers. But why should anyone vote for me?"

O.T. was making frantic gestures, and Gail almost laughed as she realized he thought the egg was breakable.

She held the egg up so everyone could see it. "I've learned a lot since the day somebody put an egg in my chair as a joke. I was wearing this feedsack dress the day I sat on the egg, and it became a symbol of everything I didn't like about this school."

She tossed the egg a foot in the air and caught it in her cupped hands. "It symbolized the algebra problems I couldn't work, the volleyballs I couldn't return, the Jail I had to stay in all lunch hour, the activities I couldn't take part in because I had to catch the bus. Most of all it was the people who made fun of me because of this dress."

No one made a sound. Red nodded encouragement.

"Then new friends helped me learn to play volleyball. All this week old and new friends helped me campaign to change things. I saw that only a few snobs care more about the clothes I wear than the things I do."

Chapter Nineteen

She met Veronica's eyes as Red and O.T. led solid applause.

Gail held the egg high. "This egg represents what I like about the school: the chance to learn from teachers and students and to make friends with kids who don't know 4-H stands for head, heart, health, and hands. I haven't learned to love algebra."

Someone yelled, "Me neither!"

"For centuries the egg has been a symbol of new life. It's the right symbol for the Students' Rights Party—because we're trying to bring new life to student government, something our experienced opponents haven't done."

She paused, searching for memorable words to end with. "Now you can choose our party's egg, or our opponents' chicken feed."

Applause and laughter greeted her last barb, and she went back to her chair happy to have had her say.

Phil adjourned the meeting without comment, and Gail's group gathered outside the door of the gym.

Ralph pumped her hand. "That egg was an inspiration!"

"And my lunch. Now that the speech is over, my stomach is reminding me I didn't eat."

Red rushed up. "Wow! You really gave it to Veronica." He dropped his eyes. "I don't see why you don't like your dress. I—I think it's real pretty."

Noreen winked at Gail. "Red, Gail has to run an errand after school, so Kenny and I are giving her a ride home—in his *convertible*. Want to come with us?"

"Gosh, I'd sure like to," Red said, "but I have to get on home and help with the chores."

Sure she was on a roll, Gail said, "Please, Red, come with us. We won't be more than ten minutes behind that slow bus."

Noreen's face had turned distant. "Maybe Red would rather not ride with us."

He glanced from her to Gail. "Oh, I want to," Red assured Noreen. "Heck, the cows can wait ten minutes."

They hurried to their homerooms to vote.

Mrs. Ransler waited until everyone was seated before taking the ballots from a locked box and passing them out one by one. She collected them with equal care and gave the box to O.T. and one of Veronica's friends to take to the office.

"She wasn't that careful last year," Noreen whispered to Gail. "She's got Veronica pegged."

"The question is, do fifty-nine students?"

O.T. didn't come back, and he didn't come to social studies sixth period.

When the last bell rang, Noreen, Gail, and Red dawdled outside Mrs. Ransler's room until Ralph and Wanda joined them.

"They've had time to count the ballots twice," Ralph said. "Something's up."

O.T. shuffled down the hall, his shoulders sagging.

"We lost," Gail said.

Chapter Nineteen

O.T. nodded. "I tried to talk the principal into calling for a new election because of those feedsacks they put around the table. He said he wasn't going through all that again. You came within six votes, Gail."

Wanda reacted first: "At least they didn't skunk us."

"Right," Red said, his lips in a false smile. "Now they know they can't run things just to suit themselves."

Ralph squared his thin shoulders. "We didn't win, but I don't feel like a loser."

"I do." Gail hadn't realized how much she'd wanted to beat Veronica, for the good guys to win against all odds.

Noreen patted Gail on the shoulder. "You're not a loser. You won big when you stood up in front of the class in your feedsack dress."

Chapter Twenty

To Gail's relief, Bobby answered the phone when she called from the furniture store. She told him she would be late and cut off his questions about how she was getting home.

Kenny pulled up outside as Gail and Noreen came out of the store. The red convertible gleamed in the soft afternoon light. The photo Gail had seen had told her Kenny was cute and blond. Now she saw that a smile warmed his face, and he looked at Noreen as if she were chocolate cake with homemade ice cream.

Red greeted Kenny, but he reached out to stroke the convertible before he and Gail climbed into the back seat. Gail thought she had probably had that same look of longing on her face when she looked at the dress in Stella's Style Shop.

During the short ride downtown she dreaded carrying the box into the shop, but she turned down Noreen's offer

Chapter Twenty

to go in with her, preferring to suffer through her embarrassment alone.

Stella's automatic smile turned into a frown when she saw the box in Gail's hands. "What's the problem? I'll bet it's the zipper."

"Nothing's wrong with the dress." Gail wished her conscience would let her lie, but the truth spilled out: "I got carried away the other day. I really can't afford it, so I didn't even take it home."

Stella fingered the ornate bow. "You never opened the box, dear, and the dress is so lovely on you. Wouldn't you like to try it on for your mother? You can think about it this weekend."

Gail shook her head, afraid to trust her voice. She had expected an argument or scolding rather than kindness.

"You're Flo Albright's girl, aren't you?"

"Yes." Gail's heart sank. Now she'd have to tell her mother before someone else did. "I have to hurry. A friend is waiting to give me a ride home. Could I—please, I'd like a refund."

"If your mother sees you in this, I'm sure she'll think it's worth the egg money."

"I'm buying my clothes with my chicken money," Gail said with pride. "I really can't afford this dress. I'm sorry."

Stella opened the cash register. "You don't need to apologize for changing your mind. That's a woman's right." She sighed and shook her head. "You have no idea how many girls, even women, wear a dress and then want to bring it back. You come in and look around any time. One of these days you'll find something you can't resist."

"Thanks," Gail said, thinking that what she'd dreaded so much Stella had taken for granted. Even so, Gail wouldn't have the nerve to shop there for a long time.

She hurried out to the street where Kenny and Red had their heads stuck under the convertible's hood. "It won't take me five minutes to buy the coat," Gail said.

"No sweat," Kenny answered without raising his head.

"I'll help you find the coat," Noreen offered.

This time Gail welcomed the company. As they hurried into the department store, she said, "He's awfully cute, Noreen, and he's obviously crazy about you."

Noreen smiled. She looked happier than any time since the Raiders had won.

When they reached the coat section, Gail went to the rack with her size. "Oh, no! They don't have any of the navy blue ones left! Just this ugly green."

"Don't panic. Maybe someone put one back in the wrong place." Noreen started examining size tags. "Here! Try this one."

Gail slipped on the coat and walked to the mirror.

Noreen followed. "It's a little big."

"It has to last at least two years, and I'm still growing." She checked the sleeves and hem to see if they could be taken up. "It should be okay."

Chapter Twenty

"Turn around slowly and let me look at it," Noreen ordered.

Gail, who had never shopped for clothes with anyone except her mother, liked having a friend's opinion.

"Now walk down the aisle and come back," Noreen said.

When Gail walked back to her, Noreen nodded approvingly. "The color and style are good for you. Your mother sews really well. I bet she can make the alterations with no problem."

Gail relaxed as she paid for the coat and calculated that she had enough left for jeans.

On the drive to the Albright farm, Kenny and Red continued to talk about the car, shouting to keep the wind from carrying their words away.

When Kenny turned into the driveway leading into the barn lot, Gail tried to see her home with Noreen and Kenny's eyes. The white frame house and green-shingled roof looked neat and cheerful. Bobby had just mowed the grass in the front yard, and yellow-orange chrysanthemums were blooming by the wire fence that separated the yard from the barn lot.

"It looks homey," Noreen said, her face wistful.

It reminded Gail how small her problems were compared to Noreen's. "Thanks heaps for the ride, Kenny. I loved it." She knew Red needed to go on home, but it didn't seem right not to offer them anything. "Would you like to come in for a glass of milk or some Kool-Aid?"

"Another time," Noreen said. "We promised we'd get this cowboy to his cows."

"Another time," Gail said to herself as Kenny backed out onto the road and took off spraying gravel. Being friends with Noreen at school was one thing. Her folks didn't need to know about that. They'd never let her go out driving, or anywhere else, with Noreen and Kenny, or anyone else, until she started to high school.

Her mother hurried toward her from the henhouse with a basket of eggs. She'd obviously done one of Gail's chores. "Wasn't that the Boyle girl and her boyfriend?"

Hoping to avoid a lecture or a direct order to stay away from Noreen, Gail held up the box. "Yes. We had election stuff at noon. Noreen offered me a ride so I could buy the coat after school."

They walked together toward the back door.

After a moment, Gail's mother said, "How did the election go?"

Gail couldn't hide her disappointment. "We lost by six votes." But O.T. hadn't said how many votes Ralph and Wanda got. "Or at least I did."

Her mother patted her on the shoulder. "You did real well, sweetheart. No new student could beat the Holt girl." She opened the screen door. "I've got something to cheer you up. Your Aunt Ellen sent you an awful nice outfit."

"She's a little late," Gail said before she thought. "Umm—I mean, it would have been nice to have something

Chapter Twenty

new to wear today."

"I know, but your father—well, that's the way things are." She put her egg basket on the kitchen table and led the way into Gail's bedroom. Opening the wardrobe, she took out a full red skirt. "Try this on and then we'll see what I need to do to the coat."

"The skirt's really pretty," Gail said, relieved that it looked brand new. "But I don't have anything to wear with it."

Her mother smiled and pulled out a short-sleeved white blouse with a thin line of red trim around the Peter Pan collar. She hung it on the door hook and reached back in for a long-sleeved white blouse with red polka dots that matched the skirt. "Aren't they lovely? And all as good as new." Her smile vanished. "Ellen had a fit when she heard you were wearing a feedsack dress to junior high."

Seeing an opportunity to come clean, Gail said, "Hardly anybody wears them. I almost bought a dress at Stella's to wear for the speech with my winter coat money."

Her mother's mouth opened in surprise.

Gail rushed on. "Of course I didn't. I can't wait to try on Aunt Ellen's stuff."

Her mother handed her the skirt. "I took up the waistband this afternoon. I think the length may be okay. Ellen is about your height."

To Gail's relief, the clothes fit reasonably well. No one except Alice would know they were hand-me-downs. "I'll wear the skirt with the polka dot blouse Monday," she said. Losers, she reflected, needed to look like winners.

Monday morning, not even the new clothes could make Gail forget her defeat and the fact that everyone she met would know about it. They'd be making fun of her or, even worse, feeling sorry for her.

To her surprise, the senior high students on the bus congratulated her on showing what country kids could do. On Friday, the high school paper had printed the Students' Bill of Rights with an editorial on how all elections should deal with genuine issues.

Buoyed by that development, she was able to keep a real smile on her face as she walked through the hall to homeroom. There Phil elbowed his way past O.T. and stuck out his hand. "Great campaign, Gail. I almost voted for you myself after that speech you made."

Gail took his hand rather than make a big deal of it, but she couldn't forget he'd taken jabs at her, including those feedsacks. She didn't trust herself to reply.

Veronica, in her chair, turned away from friends to say, "Congratulations on your campaign, Gail. I hope you'll serve on one of my committees."

Gail stared at her in disbelief. The last thing she wanted was to work with Veronica. Aware Mrs. Ransler was listening, Gail stammered, "Congratulations on your election."

She checked her chair and sank into it.

Chapter Twenty

O.T. thrust a copy of the high school newspaper into her hands. "Did you know the great gods of high school noticed us? Too bad this didn't come out before the vote." He leaned close. "I wouldn't take any committee assignments from Miss Sweetness and Mr. Light until we figure out what they're up to."

Gail whispered, "Maybe the principal told Veronica to put me on a committee."

O.T. grinned. "I doubt it. You're not one of his all-time favorites."

As the final bell rang, Noreen rushed in waving a copy of the high school paper. "Nice outfit," she said as she slid into place.

Mrs. Ransler took the roll and read the election results. "This campaign had many of the same elements as a general election, including some regrettable mudslinging. I'm sure you've all learned important lessons. Veronica, Phil, Linda, you have a responsibility to serve all the ninth graders. Gail, you and your running mates, the loyal opposition, also have a responsibility—to help those elected serve well. It's time to put aside any bad feelings that may have festered during the campaign and work together."

"Of course, Mrs. Ransler," Veronica said. "I'm inviting them all to serve on my committees."

Gail gritted her teeth in frustration. She pictured slapping Veronica. With that image in her head, she was able to smile.

"That's the spirit," the teacher said. "Noreen, is there something in that newspaper you want to share with everyone?"

"I'd be glad to." Noreen held up the paper. "The high school paper has an editorial that says the students who wrote the Students' Bill of Rights are the kinds of leaders every class should have. And ours will—after the next election."

Mrs. Ransler held up a restraining hand. "Noreen, it's too early to start the sophomore campaign. It's time for the five radio panelists to concentrate on the show. We record next Saturday morning. I want the panelists to meet in my room at noon tomorrow to test their first drafts and on Thursday for final rehearsal."

Gail sighed. She'd forgotten all about her five-minute speech on the amendments no one could remember. She still hadn't thought of anything interesting to say about them. During every class she tried to find a moment to work on the speech, but she sensed teachers' and students' eyes on her. By the end of the day she was exhausted from being the center of attention, keeping a smile on her face, saying something friendly to kids she didn't know but who now knew her.

When the bus finally dropped her off, she ran into the house to change. Having managed to keep from getting pencil marks or dirt on the glistening white blouse, she longed for the freedom to be careless. She grabbed an apple fresh from their tree and headed for the privacy of the corncrib to think about her speech.

Chapter Twenty

Her mother interrupted her before she finished shelling her first ear. "Gail—Gail! What's the matter? I've been calling you."

"I didn't hear you. I was thinking about the radio show."

"This is as good a place to talk as any." Her mother upended a galvanized bucket and sat on it. "Your father and I talked about your riding home with the Boyle girl."

Gail stopped shelling. She rarely questioned her parents' judgment, but they just didn't know the people they were judging. "Noreen is my friend, my *good* friend," Gail said quietly but firmly. "She worked darn hard on my campaign, and it was nice of her to offer me that ride. I haven't told you about it, but Veronica Holt has been really nasty to me. Things would have been lots worse if Noreen hadn't helped me."

Her mother picked up an ear and began to shell corn into her lap. "I see." She tossed a handful of grain into Gail's bucket. "Still, convertibles aren't safe, and you're too young. We don't want you runnin' around with girls who—who date older boys."

"That's not fair! All you know about Noreen is some stupid gossip. Did you know that she could've stayed with her sister in California? Instead she came back here so her father wouldn't be alone. That's the kind of person she is."

"Gail, we just don't want you to get hurt. Noreen may be a goodhearted girl, but I'm afraid she's headed for trouble. She's acting the same way her sister did. She had to get married when the boy came home last Christmas."

Gail slung her empty cob against the wall of the cornshed. "Then Noreen needs friends to help keep her out of trouble. Isn't being a friend the right thing to do?"

Mother and daughter faced off, their blue-violet eyes unwavering.

Gail's mother blinked first. "Okay, but promise me you'll tell me if she needs help. The poor girl has no family other than her drunken father to turn to."

Gail nodded. "Thanks for understanding, Mom."

Her mother got up. "I've never let other people choose my friends, and I trust your judgment more than gossip. I'll talk to your father about it." She paused at the door to the shed. "I wish you'd told me before how bad the Holt girl was. It may be hard to believe, but I was a teenager once myself. I might even have some ideas on how to deal with her."

"Thanks, Mom." Gail appreciated her mother's words, but doubted that she'd ever had to deal with kids like Veronica and Linda.

Gail shelled corn and thought about her speech and how many people would hear her on the radio. This time what she wore wouldn't matter. This time she and Veronica—all five of them—would start out even. No one would win or lose exactly, but all the ninth graders would be comparing how well all five of them did. Gail had to show that a girl who wore a feedsack dress could do just as well as the town kids.

This time she must not fail.

Chapter Twenty-one

By the time Gail got ready for bed, she had rewritten her speech six times and was sure it bordered on brilliant. By the time the radio panel met at noon, she hoped she wouldn't make a fool of herself.

They pushed the front-row chairs in Mrs. Ransler's room into a semicircle and opened their lunch bags before starting rehearsal. Everyone but Gail and Noreen had brought a thermos with soup. Gail wished she had a quiet banana instead of a noisy apple for dessert.

As chairman, Ralph introduced the topic and the speakers. He had the words right, but he read them with little expression and poor timing. Twice his voice jumped from tenor to alto.

"A good start," Mrs. Ransler told him. "You need some work on presentation." She looked at Noreen. "Perhaps someone on the panel will volunteer to help you."

Noreen blinked in surprise and then shrugged. "Sure. Why not? Why don't you come over after supper, Ralph? We'll rehearse together."

Arthur cleared his throat. "I'd like to join you, if you don't mind."

Noreen glared at him. "You gotta lot of nerve, twerp!"

Mrs. Ransler sighed. "The election is over. It's time to forgive and forget."

"After all the things they pulled?" Noreen looked straight at Veronica. "I'm not taking any more of their garbage, and I won't help any of them."

Arthur's face turned salmon pink. "I just served on the nominating committee. I didn't have anything to do with those lousy posters and slam books. I swear!"

Noreen and Ralph exchanged looks, and he answered. "Okay, Artie. Mudslinging has never been your style. It's fine with me if Noreen doesn't mind."

Veronica hadn't said a word since the group came into the classroom. Now she said, "I'll help you, Arthur."

He jammed his hands in his pockets and lowered his head. "Thanks, Veronica, but I live next door to Ralph, you know. It'll be easy for us to practice together."

Gail dropped her head to hide her triumph at Arthur's defection.

"Suit yourself!" Veronica snapped, her cheeks turning as pink as Arthur's. "Mrs. Ransler, may I give my speech on

Chapter Twenty-one

the first two amendments now?"

"Yes, let's get on with it. We have only half an hour left."

Because each student had exactly five minutes, Mrs. Ransler said they had to read their speeches. Unlike Ralph, Veronica read well, but she covered only the responsibilities that come with the right of free speech and press, ignoring freedom of religion and the rights to assemble peaceably and to bear arms.

Gail guessed that Veronica wanted to defend her own abuse of free speech and ignore a right related to her election opponents' emphasis on being allowed out of Jail at noon. For a moment she considered questioning Veronica's focus on only one right, but she decided to leave that hot potato in Mrs. Ransler's hands.

When Veronica finished, Mrs. Ransler glanced around for comments. None came. Finally she said, "That's fine, Veronica, considering the time limitations. Next."

Arthur obviously had worked hard on interpreting citizens' responsibilities related to searches and seizures, but Gail had to suppress a yawn as his voice hummed along on one note for exactly five minutes.

"Thoughtful work," Mrs. Ransler said, "and I'm sure Noreen can help you improve your delivery. Noreen, let's hear what you have to say about citizens' responsibilities and the fifth and sixth amendments."

Noreen read her speech as though she were talking

to a friend. Her voice carried conviction as she emphasized the importance of assuming people are innocent until evidence proves otherwise.

Ralph groaned as she finished. "Gee whiz! I'm going to sound like Mickey Mouse after that. Noreen sounds like an announcer." He launched into his speech. Like Arthur, he had good content and terrible delivery.

Gail gave thanks that she followed Ralph instead of Noreen. She hadn't realized before what a nice voice Noreen had. Arthur and Ralph were awful speakers, but they sounded smart. Gail worried that her talk would seem too simple in comparison.

"Let's go, Gail," Mrs. Ransler prodded. "We saw last Friday what a good speaker you are. Give us the big finish."

Picking up her note cards, Gail wriggled her shoulders to relax her taut muscles. "We don't hear much about the ninth and tenth amendments. They read like afterthoughts that say: 'And any rights we forgot to mention.' These amendments make sure that the people and the states have rights not spelled out in the Constitution or the other amendments. We can think of these as the rights to life, liberty, and the pursuit of happiness that Thomas Jefferson called for in the Declaration of Independence. The last two amendments guarantee us rights no one dreamed of back in 1788. Owning a radio, or a radio station, is an example."

Reading the words aloud, Gail heard them as stiff and textbookish. She glanced up to check reactions. Veronica

Chapter Twenty-one

had propped a pocket mirror against her thermos and was brushing her hair.

Noreen nodded encouragement.

That made Gail even more insecure. She hurried on. "Since these rights aren't listed, how can we list our responsibilities? Common sense says we the people are responsible for preserving the rights guaranteed in the Declaration, the Constitution, and the Bill of Rights. We the people also are responsible for expanding those rights, as we did with the amendments abolishing slavery and giving women the right to vote."

She paused and took a deep breath. She had reached the part of the speech with her own ideas, the part that would determine whether she'd hit a homer or struck out. She regretted eating lunch.

"We also have individual responsibilities. I've put these in five categories, each one dependent on the others.

"The first is responsibility for self. We each should strive to be economically self-reliant, to do our best not to be a burden on our family and friends or on society. More than that, we should develop our abilities so that we can better our own lives and contribute to the country's general welfare.

"The second responsibility is for family. We each must help our own family function as an economic, social, and emotional unit."

Mrs. Ransler was leaning forward, her face intent. Gail couldn't guess what the teacher was thinking.

Gail wiped away a bead of sweat trickling down her nose. "The third responsibility is for our local community. We must work with our neighbors, our fellow workers, or our classmates to make life better for everyone."

Ralph gave her a thumbs-up.

"The fourth responsibility is for our political community—our district, city, county, and state. It's not enough to vote or to pay taxes to support the schools. We need to serve in a personal way—as a class officer, a 4-H leader, a county fair board member, part of the clean-up committee after the Independence Day parade."

Gail had felt proud as she had written the words the night before. Now doubt lodged in her throat like a catfish bone. She forced out her conclusion: "If we meet these four responsibilities, then surely we meet the last one—for our country. Millions of Americans gave their lives during World War II, but that isn't the only way we serve. We have opportunities every day to make the Bill of Rights work for each of us and for all of us."

Mrs. Ransler nodded. "A nice conclusion to the entire panel, Gail. All you need to do now is practice speaking naturally rather than reading your speech."

Gail envisioned herself back at the cornsheller rehearsing.

Veronica put her brush into her purse. "I have some news. I've persuaded my grandfather to sponsor a half-hour radio program for young people every Saturday morning. If

Chapter Twenty-one

we take a few seconds from everyone's speech, I can announce it."

Five voices interrupted her, all voicing disapproval.

Veronica held up her hands in defeat. "Okay, but since this is a program about citizenship, at least give me a minute or two to discuss the class officers' plans."

Gail saw that everyone was waiting to hear what she would say. "I don't think we have time to spare. We've all worked hard to cut our speeches to five minutes."

Ralph tossed his lunch sack into the trashcan. "I think Gail's speech should be the last word."

Veronica scowled and said, "Why should—"

Noreen interrupted her. "I think so, too, Ralph. Gail ties everything up."

The bell rang.

Mrs. Ransler shooed them out the door. "I'm proud of all of you. Don't forget to bring your lunch again on Thursday for the final rehearsal."

After school that day and the next Gail rehearsed while gathering eggs, pumping water for the cows, and getting ready for bed. She envied Ralph and Arthur the chance to work, and have fun, with Noreen after school. Gail hated that *she* had to get on the bus every night, until she remembered that was her best chance to spend time with Red.

By the time the panel gathered again on Thursday, she knew every word of her speech by heart.

It didn't help. She was the only one who didn't sound

better than she had during the first rehearsal, and she talked faster so she came out twenty seconds short.

"I think you've over-rehearsed," Mrs. Ransler told her.

"It's a lot like telling an old joke," Noreen said. "You've told it a dozen times, but every time you make it sound new. You can do that, Gail. Just take it easy."

Veronica shifted impatiently in her chair. "Give Gail your pearls of wisdom some other time. Ralph, I call for a vote on giving me a couple of minutes of air time to talk about my plans for our class."

Aware Mrs. Ransler was watching, Gail bit back an angry response and tried to think of a tactful way to say what she thought of Veronica's new bid for attention.

Arthur cleared his throat, but he looked at the floor rather than at the others as he said, "I think we should vote on it again. After all, she is the class president, and elections are the foundation of a democracy."

Noreen glared at him and said something under her breath.

Ralph shrugged. "I can't argue about the importance of elections." He stuck his hands in his trouser pockets. "All in favor of giving Veronica two minutes, raise your right hand."

Gail couldn't hide a grin at Ralph's obvious sign of his vote.

Veronica raised her hand. She glared at Arthur, whose hands remained at his side. "Arthur!"

He didn't look up. "I called for a vote. I didn't promise

Chapter Twenty-one

to vote with you."

"All opposed," Ralph called.

Gail, Noreen, and Ralph raised their hands.

Veronica stuck out her lower lip. "Mrs. Ransler, this isn't fair. They're voting against me because they lost the election."

The teacher's face remained neutral. "It was decided by a majority vote, just as you requested." The bell rang. "Everyone be at the radio station ready to record at ten o'clock Saturday morning. And I expect you to all act like—good citizens."

Chapter Twenty-two

When Gail got up and went into the kitchen Saturday morning, her mother had stretched the new polka dot blouse over the end of the ironing board and was lifting the heavy iron off the top of the wood stove where it had been heating.

"I thought you'd want to dress up for the radio show," she said. She sat the iron at the wide end of the ironing board, dipped her fingers into a pan of water on the kitchen table, and sprinkled the blouse. "I won't make you wear the feedsack dress this time, or any other time. Honey, I feel so bad that I didn't realize . . ."

"It's okay." Gail hurt for her mother. To make her feel better, Gail said. "I want to wear the morning glory dress today." She searched for a believable reason. "Mr. Holt asked me to wear it."

"Are you sure you don't mind?"

Chapter Twenty-two

Gail hesitated, but she cheered up as she thought how Veronica would hate to hear her grandfather say something nice about Gail's dress. "It's been my big-event dress since school started. Why change now?"

The Albrights got to the station at 9:45, but Veronica and her grandfather already sat in the small reception room. Mr. Crystall, the station owner, stood at the door of his glass-walled office talking to them.

"The citizenship program was already planned, of course, so I can't talk about my plans here," Veronica said, ignoring the Albrights. "But I wonder if you would like to talk to me two or three minutes on your wonderful man-on-the-street program this afternoon."

Before he could answer, Mr. Holt rose. "Ain't it a fine day, folks? By golly, Gail, you're a walkin' advertisement for feedsack dresses."

Veronica's smile disappeared and her cheeks reddened.

Seeing her embarrassment, Gail remembered Veronica's quick denial at the feedstore that she would ever wear feedsack clothes. Gail wondered if Veronica made fun of feedsack dresses so everyone would know *she* didn't wear them. Was she afraid kids would make fun of her because her grandfather wore overalls like the farmers and said *ain't* and *walkin'*? Gail couldn't believe pretty, smart, popular Veronica felt insecure or ashamed of a nice man like him.

Mr. Holt shook hands with Gail's father. "Jim, this is

The Feedsack Dress

the Albrights—Flo, Simon, Gail, and Bobby. I've known this young lady since she was knee-high to a grasshopper. I'm almost as proud of her as I am of my granddaughter."

Veronica ducked her head.

Mr. Crystall stepped forward and extended his hand to Gail's father. "Pleased to meet you." He smiled at Gail. "The other candidate for class president. Elaine Ransler told me your class had a real issue-driven election." He turned to Veronica. "I read the Students' Bill of Rights in the high school paper, Veronica. A mature and courageous stand."

Gail swallowed a laugh as dismay covered Veronica's face. "Actually, sir," Gail said, "that was my party's platform."

The door opened and the rest of the panel and Mrs. Ransler came into the small lobby.

Veronica ignored them and smiled at the station owner. "That Bill of Rights was a nice dream, but pretty unrealistic."

To Gail's surprise and delight, Red stepped from behind Ralph and treated Gail to his banana grin.

Mr. Crystall turned back to Gail. "I gather that you don't agree. What are you going to do to make this 'unrealistic dream' come true?"

"We're not sure yet," Gail said, forcing herself to pay attention to him rather than Red. "We haven't given up just because we lost the election. The problems are the same no matter who's class president. We'll look for ways to get those rights."

"Good!" He beamed at both girls. "You know, I

Chapter Twenty-two

believe I'd like to try something. If you two girls can stay for an hour or so after we've recorded the citizenship panel, I'd like to interview you. We'll talk about how you plan to put what you're learning at school into practice, what the president and the minority leader will be doing."

Veronica beamed back. "What a wonderful idea! Of course, Gail hasn't thought about this as much as I have. She may not be ready."

"Gail's ready," Noreen said, her voice sharp. "You know how quick she is, Veronica."

Ralph nudged Noreen. "Great idea, Mr. Crystall. Citizenship in action, not just in theory. Everybody will listen to that."

"Then it's settled?"

Gail looked at her father. She knew he wanted to get home to put some new shingles on the henhouse roof, but he nodded, pride on his face. "I can stay," she said, though she didn't feel as ready to go on the air as Noreen had said. "Could I have a few minutes with my team before the interview show?"

Mr. Crystall chuckled. "So this is a team effort. Yes, I think we can give you a few minutes to huddle after the citizenship show." He opened a door across from his office. "The studio can hold only the five panelists, but I'll turn on the speaker so the rest of you can hear."

As the others filed in, Gail hung back to speak to Red. "How did you get here?"

"My mother has a doctor's appointment. They

dropped me off to work with Ralph on our science project." He grinned. "We'll do that later."

"I'm glad you came," she said, knowing he had to have done some pretty fancy talking to get the day off from chores. He'd proved he really liked her.

Gail's whole body felt a giant blush as she went into the studio, a room no bigger than Mrs. Ransler's storage room. The top halves of the wall by the lobby and the wall across from it were glass. A floor microphone stood by the far wall. In the middle was a small table with four folding chairs.

"You'll have to be very quiet while each person is speaking," Mr. Crystall said. "We'll turn off the tape between speakers when you change places. Our sound man in the control room," he pointed to a man sitting behind the glass wall, "will signal when he's ready for you to begin."

After testing their voices and instructing each person where to stand while speaking, he left the studio and went into the control room. The sound man motioned for Ralph to start.

Gail's stomach was doing flip-flops, but when she looked around everyone else seemed so calm. Then she noticed Noreen's grip on a pencil. Gail reached over and took it from her.

Noreen grinned and mouthed a thanks.

The five went through their speeches with few stammers and stumbles. Mr. Crystall stopped the tape to re-record Ralph once when his voice changed octaves and Arthur once when

Chapter Twenty-two

he stumbled over his words.

Gail had timed herself using the second hand on her father's pocket watch, and she kept an eye on the wall clock as she gave her speech. She almost panicked halfway through as she saw she was running fifteen seconds ahead, but she managed to slow down and come out only ten seconds short. She relaxed, feeling she had held her own.

"A fine job," Mr. Crystall assured them from the booth. "We don't need a second run-through. I wasn't too sure about this, but you've convinced me that having a student radio show is a good idea. Gail, you have half an hour before the interview to consult your advisers."

As the students came out of the studio, their listeners applauded.

Harry Holt put his hand out to Gail just as he had her father, something he'd never done before. "I sure liked what you said. You're a fine representative of the people who buy my feed. Why, I feel almost as proud of you as I do my own granddaughter. She told me you're on one of her committees. I'm real glad you'll be working with her."

"Thank you," Gail said. She couldn't tell this nice man she hated the idea of being around, let alone working with, his awful granddaughter. Obviously he had no idea Veronica hated her and made fun of her for wearing a feedsack dress.

Gail glanced at Veronica, wondering how she liked her grandfather's words.

A strained smile on her lips, Veronica turned to say

something to Mrs. Ransler.

"Come on," Noreen said. "We haven't got much time."

All the students except Veronica hurried outside to the parking lot.

Noreen frowned at Arthur. "Just a minute. Aren't you forgetting you're on the other side?"

He squared his shoulders. "I got a copy of your Students' Bill of Rights with me. You need that. Besides, whatever you decide, Gail is going to tell everyone on the radio. Gail, you said the problems are the same no matter who's president. Don't you think it would be better for us to work together rather than against each other?"

The others looked at Gail for the decision. Although suspecting Arthur's loyalties went to the last person he talked to, she said, "Okay."

Arthur pulled a piece of paper out of his pocket. He grinned. "Red suggested I study it."

"You bet I did," Red said.

His arm brushed Gail's as he spoke, and she remembered how he had been careful to stay far enough away from her to avoiding touching at the fairgrounds. Now Bobby would be right when he said Red was her boyfriend.

Ralph took the paper. "We better decide the two or three most important ones to work on first."

"Ones we have a chance with," Noreen said.

Gail nodded. "Ones that will get lots of student support and not upset the teachers." She laughed. "Anything we

Chapter Twenty-two

do probably will upset Mr. Addison."

Choosing the rights was easy. Figuring out how to get them accepted was hard. As everyone spouted ideas, Gail noticed that one of the best came from Arthur.

Mrs. Ransler stood talking to Gail's mother at the station door. When the teacher called that time was up, Noreen patted Gail on the shoulder and said, "Go get that you-know-what. You can do it."

Red whispered, "Show her what us feedsacks can do."

Gail nodded and waved him to go ahead. She wanted a moment to check the notes she had scribbled on the back of the Students' Bill of Rights.

Her mother closed the door behind the others and walked toward her. "Honey, Mrs. Ransler told me you're one of her best students. She said I should be proud of the way you've helped Noreen. She lost interest in school when her sister left and wasn't doing nearly as well as she can, but she's doing much better work lately."

"I'm so glad! She's helped me an awful lot. It's great that I've helped her."

Her mother stepped closer. "Mrs. Ransler doesn't think the stories about Noreen, uh, being fast, are true, but she worries about what will happen if everyone treats her like a—a bad girl."

Bobby skipped out the door and ran up to them. "Something's up. Mr. Crystall is talking to Mrs. Ransler and Mr. Holt in the control room where that snot Veronica can't hear."

Gail smiled at Bobby's accurate reading of Veronica. "Mr. Holt is going to sponsor a radio show for students. Maybe the owner wanted to ask Mrs. Ransler whether she thinks Veronica can do the whole show herself. I'm sure Veronica thinks she can."

Mrs. Ransler opened the door. "Show time, Gail."

As Gail reached her, the teacher whispered, "No matter what Veronica says, don't lose your temper. Use your brain before you do your tongue."

Blushing as she recognized that she'd earned the teacher's warning, Gail vowed to rein in her temper no matter what manure Veronica threw at her.

Aloud the teacher added, "Don't be nervous. You speak very well without a script."

Gail's father laughed. "Gail's never had trouble comin' up with somethin' to say, has she, Harry?"

"Not since she was two," the feedstore owner agreed. "Veronica's the same way."

Ushering Gail and Veronica into the studio, Mr. Crystall placed them in chairs across the table from him. A mike sat on each side of the table.

"Okay, girls, just relax," he said. "First, I'll give a short introduction. Next I'll ask Veronica a few questions about her plans as president. Then I'll ask Gail her plans for the Students' Bill of Rights." He glanced toward the control room, and the sound man nodded. "I'm not going to baby you.

Chapter Twenty-two

Some of my questions will be tough, but I know you two can handle them. If something really throws you, we can turn off the tape."

They nodded, and Veronica put several note cards on the table.

Gail smoothed out her crumpled sheet and studied it as Mr. Crystall introduced both girls and explained that they had been opponents in a close class election. She abandoned her notes as soon as he spoke to Veronica.

"Veronica, I understand that Gail's Student Rights party had a very appealing platform, the Students' Bill of Rights. How did you campaign against that?"

Uncertainty flashed on Veronica's face. "I—uh—I ran on my record. I—all three candidates on my ticket—have lots of experience in student government. Our fellow students knew we would continue to give them good government."

"Tell us a little about what you had already accomplished as a class officer."

Veronica smiled confidently. "Our spring party last year was one of the best ever. It was the first time an eighth graders' dance had a live band instead of just records. I added a lot of social activities last year, and I'm planning a really super Halloween party."

"What have you planned for your presidential term beside social events?"

"I will work with the faculty in dividing up the money for extracurricular activities—dances and clubs and intramural sports. And I'm working with a committee to recommend activities for next year's freshman class. Naturally, part of my duties will be to represent the class at the school and in the community."

He turned to Gail. "As the co-author of the Students' Bill of Rights, Gail, what are your plans for the year?"

"My slate—Ralph Toffani, Wanda Ruckles, and I—and our supporters will work to get those rights, starting with the ones we think are most important and affect the most students."

"Didn't the students indicate a lack of interest in those rights when they voted against you?"

Veronica nodded and smirked.

Gail conquered her anger by concentrating on what Mr. Crystall had asked. "Not really. We started gaining support when we announced the Students' Bill of Rights, which is based, of course, on the Constitution's Bill of Rights." Honesty compelled her to add, "My defeat was a personal failure rather than a rejection of our ideas. As Veronica said, her slate had more experience than ours." And a heck of a lot more nerve, she added to herself.

"So you take personal responsibility for your defeat?"

The misery of losing swept over Gail. "Yes."

Mr. Crystall laughed. "You're the first defeated candidate I've ever interviewed who doesn't have a full set of excuses. I can see why you have such devoted supporters. Tell us what you and your team plan to do this year."

Chapter Twenty-two

His warm smile encouraged Gail. "We haven't planned it all yet, but we'll begin by circulating a petition among all the junior high students asking for the right of peaceable assembly at noon. A lot of us bring our lunch to school, and we hate being stuck in the Jail—that's what we call the lunchroom—the whole noon hour. We want to be able to go read in the library, play games in the gym, and go outside to make a call or buy a candy bar."

He moved the mike toward Veronica. "Will you sign that petition?"

Veronica's lips smiled, but her eyes didn't. "This is the first I've heard of it. I'll have to read it before I decide."

"What will your next step be, Gail?"

To show everyone Veronica and her crowd can't bully us, she thought, but said, "We're going to circulate a petition calling for a vote on extracurricular activities. Some of the noon activities, the ones the country kids can do, are boring and—" she searched for the right word and remembered one from a vocabulary lesson—"downright condescending. The ones that are fun come after school when lots of the kids either have to get on the bus or go home to do chores."

Out of the corner of her eye, Gail saw that Veronica was turning pink and leaning toward the mike. In the parking lot Gail had guessed what Veronica's objections to the petition would be and prepared to head her off at the pass: "Most of the activities haven't started yet, so we could switch to things kids really want right away. We don't have to wait for another year or even another semester."

Mr. Crystall gave Gail a nod of approval. "What's the president's reaction to this proposal?"

"No one will sign her silly petitions," Veronica snapped. "The students elected us, not her. We like things the way they are. The only reason she was a candidate was that no one else wanted to run against me. Her 'team' is nothing but a few troublemakers."

Gail watched Veronica's pink deepen to red. She knew she'd been caught being nasty. "I'm sorry. Could you erase that from the tape, Mr. Crystall?"

He smiled slightly. "I think that might be wise. Try again, Veronica."

Gail held her paper in front of her face to hide her triumph that Veronica had revealed her true snotty self.

Veronica pushed her hair back and leaned closer to the mike. "Gail should accept that the majority has spoken and work with me rather than against me. I'll be happy to appoint her to my committee on extracurricular activities."

He moved the mike toward Gail. "Will you serve on Veronica's committee, Gail?"

She wanted to snarl no, but she knew that would come back to haunt her. "Of course. I'll cooperate with her in any way I can." Gail doubted there would be many ways. "But I'll still circulate the petitions."

He nodded approvingly. "A politician's answer. What about the other rights in your platform?"

Chapter Twenty-two

"We'll tackle them one by one." She remembered a phrase Arthur had used. "We're drawing up a list of priorities."

"Veronica? What does the President say to this?"

She smiled sourly. "Gail and I have debated this in class and on the radio panel on citizenship. I don't think students are ready to take on the responsibilities of all these rights she wants to give them. I trust the principal and the teachers to make the right decisions for us."

Gail almost gagged. She hoped the teachers didn't buy it.

Mr. Crystall glanced at the wall clock. "It looks like an interesting year at Craigsburg Junior High. We'll be keeping track of developments there and at the senior high with a new weekly half-hour program sponsored by Holt's Feed. I think you'll be hearing again from both Veronica Holt and Gail Albright, two outstanding students who are developing their political philosophies and skills by participating in student government. This is Jim Crystall thanking you for listening."

Gail's mouth fell open. He wanted her on the radio again!

He leaned back and smiled at the girls. "You're both naturals. This will be a great way to announce the new *Students Say* program."

Gail's shoulders ached from tension. She wriggled them. "I feel like I've been shocking oats all day. Being on the radio is exhausting."

He laughed. "It's not as easy as it looks. Come out to

my office and we'll talk about your participation in *Students Say*."

As Gail stepped from the studio into the lobby, everyone called out congratulations.

Ralph said, "Artie offered to look up how to write petitions in his dad's law library. We'll be ready to start writing Monday."

"Great," Gail said. Ralph had been against using petitions, but he had accepted her decision and was ready to help.

Mr. Crystall guided both Gail and Veronica into his office.

Mr. Holt, already there, held chairs for the girls as if they were grown-ups.

The station owner leaned against a giant desk with neat little stacks of paper. "Maybe you'll want to invite the principal to be a guest on one of your shows, Gail."

Gail wasn't sure what he meant by "your" show, so she kept her mouth shut.

Just outside the door Red gave a victory whoop. "Your show, Gail. *Your* show!"

Mr. Crystall grinned at her. "If you want to do it, of course. I asked your father earlier, and he promised to get you here one Saturday morning a month. Harry and I thought you could be in charge of organizing the junior high edition and serve as moderator. Elaine—Mrs. Ransler—has agreed to be the faculty adviser."

Chapter Twenty-two

Gail was so thrilled she could only nod yes.

Tears welled up in Veronica's eyes, and she didn't try to hide them. "What about me, Grampa?"

Mr. Crystall took one huge step forward and closed the door.

"Now, sweetie pie," Mr. Holt said, surprise on his face, "you'll be on the program just like Gail's on your committee. How would it look if I put my granddaughter in charge? Remember, I'm advertisin' my business. My customers will love having a farm girl on the air."

As Veronica wiped her eyes, her grandfather looked at Gail for help.

Overcoming the desire to gloat at her unimagined triumph and remembering she had to go to school with Veronica for four more years, Gail said, "Naturally you'll be on the show with your president's report." Gail estimated two minutes a show would be plenty.

Mr. Holt patted Veronica, who was still shedding tears, on the knee. "I know my girl will help Gail make it the best student show there is."

Mr. Crystall glanced at his watch. "You can work it out, Gail. I suggest you put the Boyle girl on the air, too. Young as she is, she has a great radio voice."

"She'll have a lot of ideas, too," Gail said. She couldn't hold back a big smile as she thought how much fun they would have.

Veronica moaned.

Mr. Holt sighed. "Sweetie pie, you'll be so busy being president you wouldn't have time to run this, too."

When she didn't respond, he added, "I'm sure you'll help Gail all you can. That's the way the Holts do things."

Veronica wiped away one last tear. "I'll do it for you, Grampa."

She rose, turned so her grandfather couldn't see her face, gave Gail a hateful look, and hurried out of the office.

"This will cost me a new pair of penny loafers and a Sunday hat," Mr. Holt said, "but she'll come around. She's a good girl and smart as a whip. She'll be a big help to you."

Gail forced a smile and gave silent thanks that she had allies now.

Mr. Holt stood up slowly. "Jim will tell you what to do, Gail. I'll leave everything to him and your teacher." He walked to the door and paused. "By the way, when the newspaper takes your picture to go with the article about the new show, I'd sure appreciate it if you would wear your pretty feedsack dress."

Gail looked down at the morning glories climbing up her skirt. He was right. The feedsack dress really was pretty. It hadn't been a jinx. Her mistake had been looking at it through others' eyes.